I Wanted to be Clo

Katie Oliver

To Mike and Lesley,

Thank you so much for your support, and I hope you enjoy the book!

All the best,
Katie
KO

First published December 2022 by Fly on the Wall Press
Published in the UK by
Fly on the Wall Press
56 High Lea Rd
New Mills
Derbyshire
SK22 3DP

www.flyonthewallpress.co.uk
ISBN:978-1-913211-87-5

Copyright Katie Oliver © 2022

The right of Katie Oliver to be identified as the author of this work has been asserted in accordance with the Copyright, Designs and Patents Act 1988.

Typesetting by Isabelle Kenyon. Cover photo- Shutterstock . All rights reserved. No part of this publication may be reproduced, stored in or introduced into a retrieval system, or transmitted in any form, or by any means (electronic, mechanical, photocopying, recording or otherwise) without prior written permissions of the publisher. Any person who does any unauthorised act in relation to this publication may be liable for criminal prosecution and civil claims for damages.

A CIP Catalogue record for this book is available from the British Library.

For everyone who didn't give up.

Contents

Contents

Tending the Garden

Nella is often performatively cruel to her husband, even when—no, *especially* when—he wheels out their wedding DVD to entertain guests, for the fucking umpteenth time.

"Give it a rest Gary, no-one gives a shit," she mutters from the armchair in the corner, red wine and a cigarette on the go. Meanwhile, Gary tries to pretend he isn't embarrassed.

He really does try: for Valentine's Day he'd attempted heart-shaped cupcakes, with pink icing and sugar flowers. Cloying. Nella put them on the compost heap, to teach him a lesson. He is still paying off her engagement ring on his credit card.

She would like to leave, of course she would. Except that actually, she can't. Only Gary knows what's buried out there, festering beneath the soil. She walks a fine line between letting off steam and putting herself in danger, stamping on the carpet of eggshells in a temper and then scrambling to stick the shards back together.

"It'll be alright, Nella," he says, stroking her face in a way that makes her want to commit another murder. He squeezes her arm so hard the purple ghost of his fingertips lingers for days after. "I love you," he whispers.

They plant flowers. So many flowers, a manic trip to the garden centre resulting in a bewildering riot of colour. Buds yawn open, lascivious mouths with tongues snaking out. The red lilies had been a mistake.

They let the garden grow out of control. Wildflowers burst through tangled clouds of weeds that suffocate the neglected shop-bought blooms: poppies, crimson and fleeting, oversized daisies, bluebells. They give Nella a migraine.

It is July, and the air wavers in a haze of heat. Wearing only her underwear, Nella takes the secateurs and hacks down anything that grows with barely controlled violence. It takes a long time to destroy everything. Sweat pours down her face and mixes with tears that disappear into the earth so quickly it's as if they were never there.

All that Glitters

The water in the shower ran clear today, albeit with a strange metallic smell that made Cecilia think about the taste of blood. Still, it was an improvement; last week the water had been brown, and the week before there had been none at all. It had been a dry summer, and all the houses in the neighbourhood had received a message from the water supplier apologising for the disruption, with assurances that they were working on getting everything fixed as soon as possible. Judging by today, everything seemed fine, or fine enough. It was no secret that water supplies were dwindling, but they'd evidently come up with something, for now at least.

Cecilia inhaled deeply, letting the steam envelop her. If she ignored the smell and the black mould blooming on the bathroom ceiling, she could almost pretend she was under a waterfall, somewhere else.

Taking a shower was high on the list of Cecilia's priorities. She spent an irresponsible amount of her meagre salary on toiletries, the more luxurious and tropical-scented the better (her current shower gel was pineapple-flavoured and contained real gold). Under the comforting streams of warm water, Cecilia could be anyone. Anything. A socialite on her third Caribbean holiday of the year, rinsing white sand from her impossibly lithe body. The last blue whale in the world, filtering plankton through her teeth. A mermaid, whose silver scales lured wayward sailors to untimely death. Someone who *did* things, went places. Formed normal relationships.

The spurts of water coughed and sputtered, until eventually they stopped altogether. It was just as well, really; the metallic smell was quite unpleasant, and her skin was starting to itch. As she stepped out into the real world and began to dry off, she noticed a large patch of dry, scaly skin on her right thigh.

Never mind, she told herself encouragingly: nothing that a bit of passionfruit and papaya moisturiser couldn't fix.

It was a bad night. Cecilia itched constantly and barely slept as a consequence; woke covered in flakes of her own skin: flesh confetti. It was depressing, she mused, to witness the real-time collapse of a body.

As she dabbed moisturiser onto the offending patches, she idly scrolled through the news. Her attention was caught by an article about two little girls in the Philippines who had grown silver scales all over their legs and torsos. Overnight celebrities, with a heavily-subscribed VidiLink channel, they were being flown out to America to do a tour of the big chat shows.

REAL LIFE MERMAIDS!

Close up shots were naturally included, the shimmering gashes vivid against the girls' dark skin. The main picture showed both of them smiling directly at the camera, holding hands; the smallest one was missing a front tooth. Cecilia thought that they looked very happy. She rubbed in the last of her cream.

By the next morning it was apparent that something was most definitely amiss: the dry patches had spread so that Cecilia's legs and torso were almost totally covered. She wasn't at all prone to strong emotions, finding them unnecessarily tiring; even so, she felt an undeniable sense of panic. She knew that she was reaching the sell-by-date on her looks, but at thirty-seven she wasn't *quite* yet ready to admit defeat.

Experimentally, she began to peel one of the longer strips of skin on her thigh; the curl of shrivelled tissue was tacky yet crisp around the edges, like a smear of glue not yet solidified. The top layer came away easily enough, leaving some smaller wisps of skin, and revealing an unmistakable flash of silver. She rubbed at the patch slowly, then with increasing urgency. The more she scrubbed, the brighter it shone. It had an other-worldly quality, shiny and pearlescent. It glittered.

Compelled, Cecilia lurched out of bed to get her tablet, where she hurriedly brought up the article from yesterday. She pressed one of the silver patches on her thigh and felt a connection with the little girls smiling halfway across the world.

From the moment Cecilia tentatively set up a LyfeShare account and uploaded her first picture, things happened with dizzying speed. She'd felt the need to tell someone, anyone, what was happening to her, and it wasn't as if there was an abundance of friends and family crowding around to listen. The full-length mirror shot that showed off her almost totally silver legs and scaled torso marked her out as one of the more extreme cases, and interest was frenzied. The flurry of likes and shares the picture garnered resulted in over two thousand followers almost immediately, much to her shock and—she admitted it—delight. The tabloids quickly picked up the picture and produced articles (in the loosest sense of the term) that were light on fact and leaden with aggressive formatting.

Mermaids DO exist! Blonde bombshell Cecilia, 37, is UK's FIRST case of Glitter Scales.

That was what they were calling it: Glitter Scales. Of course, scientists had come up with a fancy Latin name, but most people weren't going to bother with that. Besides, Glitter Scales sounded cute, like something a six-year-old girl might be obsessed with, or a make-up trend that a LyfeSharer Platinum Plus might wear at a festival.

Suddenly, Cecilia's life was fuller than it had ever been, times a thousand. A constant stream of online adulation, amazement, abuse. There were daily requests for interviews and chat shows, and she appeared on the news with a celebrity scientist. An offhand mention of her love for all things tropical resulted in an industriously buzzing drone at her front door eight hours later, bearing a month's supply of Guava Crush hair products (*Take your hair on holiday!*). For the first time in her slightly disappointing life, Cecilia was *someone*, a Person Of Note. It almost felt like she had friends, or something like it, if she ignored the online death threats. She only had to post a couple of meaningless words on social media and within minutes she was flooded with responses. There was noise where there had once only been a vacuum.

It didn't take very long for the deaths to start. Exactly two weeks after Cecilia first discovered her scales, the two girls from the Philippines turned yellow, then died. The following day it was the Californian pensioner, and the next it was a group of Australian farm workers and a Ukrainian basketball player. Statements were duly released by the relevant governments promising that resources were being poured into finding a solution. Regrettably, there was no known cure. People were advised to use bottled water to wash, if they could afford it—otherwise, the best hope was to wait for the rain to come and stock up on purifying tablets. If you could afford those. The full timeline of the Glitter Scales experience was still being established: for most people it was approximately three weeks after the scales appeared that the whites of the eyes and skin turned yellow, with internal bleeding following shortly after. Most died from cardiac arrest, but it was reported that one woman had choked to death after the skin inside her throat and mouth disintegrated.

The public took it hard; they had thrown themselves wholeheartedly into the Glitters' lives and felt cheated that the colourful experience would only be fleeting. Determined to squeeze every last drop from it, subscribers to the Glitters' channels and social media jumped by the thousands overnight; shrines popped up anywhere there was space for a candle—outside supermarkets, on beaches, in public toilets. There was talk of a commemorative song being recorded by a group of celebrities.

It was late afternoon: the time Cecilia usually did a live chat with her followers to let them know how her day was going. She inhaled shakily and focused on her reflection: a gnarled patchwork of silver and yellow. Her lungs clenched with the sensation she'd become horribly familiar with over the past few days. The scales at her throat shimmered, brighter than ever. She broke into another coughing fit, not bothering to turn away from the camera as blood and mucus spattered the monitor. A new comment appeared almost immediately.

thats brutal lol

Hands trembling, Cecilia reached for a wet-wipe and tried to clean the computer screen. Her earnest attempt prompted an intense flurry of likes and comments, the app on her phone buzzing angrily as they flooded in.

hun, ur so brave.
Soooooo sad! <3
How long do you think you have left?
:(
#JusticeForGlitters
fuck your an absolute freak of nature

She decided not to wipe away the blood that had begun to trickle from the corner of her mouth. She felt strangely beautiful. And satiated. Full up with all their words. She drank them in, glittering. Slipping away.

Cecilia, know that I'm praying for you. xxx
Gross
@huni237 you watching this???
Cecilia, I'm so sorry that you're experiencing this #JusticeForGlitters
There must be something they can do to help??
#JusticeForGlitters
this is so fuckin fake
Jesus will protect you Cecilia
u deserve to be raped
im gonna miss you so much C :(:(x
This is a SICK aesthetic!!!!!!!
#JusticeForGlitters
#JusticeForGlitters
#JusticeForGlitters

She had never been so popular.

Hold on Tight

An escalator is the ideal hunting ground: so many faceless bodies. It's easier, he feels, when you don't see their faces. He hops up the steps two at a time, to show he's just a regular busy guy on his way to work.

All the world is here, on this slow-moving conveyor belt. Different ages, ethnicities, body types, and he doesn't discriminate. A pat here, a squeeze there, so vanishingly light that they can barely register what's happened. When they whip their heads around he's already gone. He's well-practised: a master of his craft. And so they don't say anything. They can't be sure, and they don't want to cause a scene. Besides, what could be done?

A sudden jolt and he staggers, falls. The jagged metal teeth show him no kindness. It's a long way down. Something is broken, and blood seeps from the deep gash in his cheekbone. People step over him, because they all have places to be. He is going to miss a very important meeting.

The faceless bodies have since scaled the summit, oblivious to the cosmic meting out of justice. The next day a new sign appears, reminding commuters to *always* hold the handrail when using the escalators.

The Sanctuary

Lara's new job is going very nicely. The exact title is 'Executive Services Administrator', although she's not exactly sure what this means; it's debatable whether anyone else in the office knows either. When acquaintances enquire further, she just tells them that she works 'in admin'. She imagines 'admin' to be a giant glass bowl in which several people rattle around, scrambling fruitlessly as they attempt to scale the slippery convex edges.

The majority of Lara's colleagues are friendly, but not distressingly so. A woman named Desirée makes her a cup of tea each morning, and a man named Giles whose Adam's apple seems to have a life of its own has offered to add her to the weekly lottery syndicate.

"You never know!" he'd said, the first time they'd bumped into each other in the canteen. Lara had agreed that, indeed, you didn't.

Yes, the new job is most satisfactory, except for one small but significant issue. The woman who sits to her right, Penny, has three spider plants on her desk. On Lara's first day she gushes that she's 'bagsied' the seat by the window specifically due to a desire to maintain the aforementioned plants. And from the second Lara sits down she can hear them screaming.

It had started when she was three years old. Her grandfather had a Malabar Chestnut tree on the porch that he referred to as a money tree, and he'd hidden coins among the branches for her amusement. It had been many years before she'd realised that the tree didn't *really* sprout money. But the main thing was that the plant would let out little silvery giggles at the coin resting against its tender bark, and a sigh of relaxation when you plucked the metal away. Her grandfather was a diligent gardener, and so the tree was never in any distress. But from then on Lara could hear plants wherever she went. The worst was at school, where her peers yanked up daisies and dandelions from outdoor play areas at will and wondered why she was crying. Freshly-mown lawns were a no-go area, sodden with sweet-smelling death and the cries of the wounded. And she would never forget the time that her mother had taken her into a florist; the heavily perfumed cacophony of pain had been quite literally unbearable to experience and she'd had a small fit and been sick on the floor, much to her mother's mortification.

In search of solace, she gravitated towards forests and meadows, where plants were left to be themselves. She wrapped her arms around ancient trees who wheezed gently in the wind; sighed as poppies turned their delicate faces towards the sun. Most of all, she listened to the creak and pop of seeds as they wound their way up into the world, pressing her face to the soil with the reverence that people reserve only for the things they truly believe in.

It is Lara's third week on the job and there is a heatwave. The glass-walled, east-facing office sweats like a greenhouse, the air thick and fetid even at 8am; on Monday morning Lara feels herself drooping as soon as she steps through the door. That, however, is nothing compared to the wretched spider plants. Left unshaded and without sustenance all weekend, their pointed ends have withered into papery brown stubs and their whimpers of distress are acute. Penny types away beside them, unmoved. Lara has to work hard to swallow down the rage that rises up her oesophagus; she sometimes forgets that other people can't hear what she can. She also must remember that she is still new in this role, and she can't very well go round picking fights with her colleagues. Desirée, clearly a woman of habit, hands her a steaming cup of tea that is profoundly unappealing at this time. Lara takes it, burning her hands in the process.

"Thank you so much," she says.

"Nice weekend?" asks Penny, face screenwards.

"It was quite hot," says Lara, pointedly.

"Oh, tell me about it," says Penny, rolling her eyes. As one of the plants breaks into wracking sobs, Lara excuses herself to the bathroom where she rests her forehead against the cool of the mirror, ears still tangled with screams.

When Penny pops out to buy a Cornish pasty Lara waters the spider plants covertly, filling the little saucers in the manner of a nurse administering a drip. The sighs of relief emitting from the plants are like cool aloe coating the inside of her ears; she feels a knot of tension in her chest loosen and unfurl. The plants are already looking less tragic, but the peak of the day's heat hasn't yet been reached and Lara realises that as things stand, this can only be a brief period of respite. Ideally, she'd move the unfortunate trio to a new location entirely, but of course, doing so would only raise uncomfortable questions. She now understands how concerned bystanders must feel when trying to decide whether or not to report their neighbours to social services for child neglect.

The next couple of hours are taken up with lunch and a meeting in a different part of the building, which provides adequate distraction; it's as much as anyone can do to focus as antediluvian fans recirculate air around their inert bodies. But when Lara returns to the office it's just as bad as she'd feared, worse, even: no one had thought to close the blind and the spider plants have deteriorated further, the once-elegant foliage now more shrivelled than ever. One of the plants, the largest one, is beside itself. *He's dead! He's dead!* it shrieks on repeat, so hysterical Lara worries it might shred its own leaves in a frenzy. This is the first time she's ever been able to make out actual words. She aches to comfort it, to wrap her arms around its fragile plastic pot and tell it that she understands. The smallest plant certainly doesn't look too perky, but Lara can see that there's still some hope.

"He's not dead," she whispers, the words tumbling out of her mouth before she can stop them. Penny swivels to look at her, flakes of pasty still dusting her chin as she narrows her eyes.

"What did you say?"

"Oh—nothing," says Lara. "Song lyrics."

Penny sniffs, raises her eyebrows.

"Sounds a funny sort of song. Now, about your timesheets—"

As Penny undertakes to explain in great detail the process for submitting timesheets to HR, Lara tries to stop her eyes from flicking towards the exhausted plants who have stopped wailing, but are now maintaining a low, undulating moan that pulsates in the centre of Lara's skull to the rhythm of her heartbeat. After fifteen excruciating minutes she finally cracks.

"Your plants," she says, breathing hard.

"Sorry?" Penny is confused.

"Would you—would you not consider moving them? Out of the sun," Lara explains, her mouth dry. "They're wilting." She waits to measure the impact of her words, fixing Penny with pleading eyes. Penny smiles and tilts her head to one side.

"Oh, you're very thoughtful, dear, but those plants are tough as old boots. It'll take a lot more than a bit of sun to finish them off!" There is a sudden silence that Lara doesn't understand, until Penny squeals.

"Good Lord, Lara, there's blood coming out of your ear!"

Lara feels it flow like lava along the outline of her jaw as she slides down her spinny office chair and quietly collapses to the floor.

Regaining consciousness in the medical office, Lara understands that drastic action will have to be taken; time is of the essence and simply does not allow for her relationship with Penny to develop to such an extent that she will begin to accept advice on the wellbeing of her plants. The heatwave is forecast to continue at least until the end of the week and Lara values her eardrums far too much to delay a moment longer. With a damp flannel pressed against her forehead she decides upon kidnap; the only other option would be to simply put the plants out of their misery and both she and they are not quite yet at that stage.

The medical officer sends Lara home but instead she lurks in a stationery cupboard to wait until six o'clock, when she can have unfettered access to the office. At the allotted time, she breaks cover and runs the gamut of security guards, ducking in and out of shadows and hiding behind bins. She feels righteous, like a superhero. She is saving lives. Once back in the heavy, damp atmosphere of the office, she acts quickly, scooping the plants into a paper bag.

"I'm taking you somewhere no one can hurt you," she whispers. A small, weary cheer goes up from inside the bag. On the tube home Lara cradles the bag to her chest, adrenaline starting to abate. The plants mumble, disorientated, but the cries of distress have ceased. When she arrives home she places the plants in the kitchen, tends to them lovingly. Allows them to drink, feed. Trims the crispy bits ("this will only sting for a minute, I promise"). She sings to them.

In the morning she wakes to a phone call from her manager, Ines.

"I can't even believe I'm saying this, Lara, but you've been seen on CCTV after hours stealing Penny's spider plants. It's really erratic behaviour. Penny's going to be very upset." Lara glances towards the three fugitives, who are currently humming contentedly on her worktop.

"I didn't mean—I didn't want to upset Penny -"

"You wrote 'PLANT KILLING SCUM' on all of her post-its, Lara."

There is a long, awkward silence.

"You were doing really well, and I don't know what might be going on behind the scenes, but I'm going to have to place you on leave until further notice." Ines pauses again to see if Lara has anything to say for herself. "And I'll book you an appointment with Occupational Health."

Lara leans back on the sofa. The sound of the happy plants is a faint, harmonised angel's song; a feather caressing the string of a harp. Soft waves lapping at a shoreline. She takes in the on-sale pansies from the garden centre, the hydrangea bush dug up from a neighbour's front garden under cover of darkness, the plastic-wrapped bouquets from the garage forecourt, the storm-whipped sapling with the broken branch, the bridal posy she made sure she caught at her cousin's wedding, the limp, poignant daisy chain and the three liberated spider plants.

All safe now.

Spider Season

It's September: spider season. Summer has outstayed its welcome, the perpetual hum of winged beasts fraying her nerves as she practises looking over her shoulder again. A house spider appears first. Its web is a perfect feat of engineering that spans the width of the back door, granting her permission to remain inside.

The house spider's endorsement triggers an influx of new webs. They begin to overlap across the glass panels, tapestries of death and industry. There is a false widow that she knows she really ought to remove, but she is moved by how it scuttles into the cloud-like nest of its web as she approaches, fearful of predators. *I won't dust you away*, she promises.

The spiders grow fat on the creatures they catch, studding their gossamer cathedrals with the night's spoils. A tiny black-and-yellow corpse dangles amidst the graveyard of flies, rotating ponderously on a silken string like a warning. Instinctively, she reaches for the panic alarm in her pocket, runs her thumb over the button. Flicks a glance towards the knife block on the counter.

As the nights grow colder and the date marked with 'x' looms closer, she knits webs of fine grey wool that cascade over her knees, carpeting the floor beneath her feet. She wraps herself in one of her creations and steps onto the front porch, just for a second; the cool air brushes her face with its fingertips for the first time in weeks. Over by the back door, her miniature army spins and waits and pounces: toiling through the night, counting down the days. She pulls her web tight around her and feels the throb of venom in her jaws.

Gum Leaf Skeletoniser

The counsellor said to occupy myself with activities that were unlikely to be triggering, which is how I come to find myself reading a book entitled: *A field guide to common insects of Australia and New Zealand.*

I learn that Gum Leaf Skeletonisers are caterpillars that moult thirteen times. From the fourth time they retain the heads of their discarded exoskeletons, stacking them on top of their current heads until a tower of hollow skulls teeters over their tiny bodies. I decide that I will do the same: when a bad thought comes, I'll just moult it out, and shove the offending thing away up in my hair so it can't touch me.

The first time it happens it's a rush, my whole body tingling as a layer peels off. I scramble to balance the delicate shell on my head, black spots bursting in front of my eyes. The flashback recedes. I feel better, and moult again for good measure.

Gum Leaf Skeletonisers use the horns they make from parts of themselves to bat away predators and protect their soft, exposed flesh.

A car exhaust backfires and I almost fall into a bush. Shaking, I moult almost immediately, using both hands to steady the growing spire that makes me sway beneath its weight. Insect-small, I attempt to navigate a street that now vibrates with threat: a smashed window, heavy bootsteps. Shots fired.

Researchers have found that while Gum Leaf Skeletonisers' horns help them to fend off an assault, they ultimately only prolong the ordeal.

I trace the pitted scar on my arm, fingertips coming away bloody with memory. I squeeze my eyes tight shut.

Gum Leaf Skeletonisers will always succumb to their attackers in the end.

Underbelly

It had been a difficult birth, although Claire knew that she had no-one to blame but herself. Still, she recognised that she was fortunate: she had an extraordinarily permissive husband. Artificial wombs were popular nowadays for those who could afford it, but the all-purpose C-section was the most common method; baby out nice and quick with a tummy tuck and lipo thrown in. Everything good as new—or better, some insisted. But there were nonetheless a renegade few such as herself who insisted on doing it the old-fashioned way. It was frowned upon, certainly, but still possible with an understanding partner and a doctor who was willing to risk a lawsuit. Claire liked to think she wouldn't have even *considered* procreating with Philip if he hadn't been respectful of her wishes. They had met at a wellness retreat three years ago, and had bonded while conversing earnestly about climate change and the arms trade. They'd drunk kitsch kombucha smoothies self-consciously served in coconut shells by girls who seemed slightly too young and made Claire feel shitty about how much the retreat had cost versus how much she suspected they weren't being paid.

She was fiercely proud of herself: only gas and air despite twenty hours of labour, exactly how she'd wanted it to be. The baby had been born in a birthing pool like on one of those old videos you could watch, where the women mooed gently and expelled slow scarlet clouds of blood. The water sadly hadn't prevented a nasty second-degree tear, but Philip hadn't even complained. That was where he was different, so progressive: she couldn't imagine any of her friends encountering a similarly calm reaction. Some of them were actually extremely oppressed, although she would never have said it to their faces.

The baby was doing fine, the doctor had said, but needed some observation on his breathing. As soon as she'd delivered the placenta, they were both hurried out of the room on separate trolleys and smoothly rolled in different directions, a clinical parody of an old-style musical number. Claire was wheeled into theatre and a spinal anaesthetic was quickly administered. She was now all set up for the remodelling.

Lying prone, with her legs in stirrups, Claire was reminded of a nature documentary she'd seen a while back that had featured a dung beetle pushing a ball of excrement up a slope. It had toiled for several agonising minutes before tipping over onto its back where it kicked its many tiny legs. "*Thwarted, the beetle lies helpless, at the mercy of the elements*", intoned the narrator.

As per the most recent laws, if a woman's husband or partner consented to a vaginal delivery, they could also oversee the clean-up job, to make sure that everything was back in working order as soon as possible. It was understandably a taboo subject, and her and Philip had already agreed that they wouldn't be discussing their decision with anyone else; it wasn't exactly the sort of thing you could casually drop into conversation over brunch these days. Claire had learnt this the hard way: she hadn't forgotten the time she'd tentatively mentioned to some former colleagues that she didn't think a natural birth would be the *worst* thing in the world. The immediate appalled silence was swiftly followed by a brutal exclusion from the coffee run, and rumours had started to circulate that she was a member of a cult.

Claire was still high from the rush of giving birth and desperately wanted to see the baby, but the anaesthetic was strong and she was totally numb below the waist. She could have done with a shower as well, and some food. Instead, she contented herself with fiddling with the tags on her hospital wristband. After all, she'd willingly signed the form, and she'd known what this part would entail.

She thought back to the initial consultation they'd been to, where they'd been given the full red-carpet treatment that was designed to convince them that they could definitely trust the doctor with their money, and her body. His office was as you'd imagine a private consultant's to be: sterile, yet rich-looking. The obvious anomaly was that one of the walls was covered floor to ceiling with photographs of vulvas, each one blown up to three times its natural size. Claire was reminded of one of those art projects where two hundred different women let someone take pictures of their genitals, to reassure them that it was OK to have one labia that was drastically longer than the other or to not remove their pubic hair. It was like that, except each of the vulvas on display here was curiously uniform; in shape, size, even colour.

"Just some of my happy customers," the doctor twinkled, inclining his head towards the wall when he noted the direction of Claire's gaze.

"They're all very...similar," muttered Claire. As she squinted at one of the photographs she found herself wondering whether it was computer generated.

"Thank you!" replied the doctor, delighted. "Yes, we've had excellent results with bleaching techniques to ensure a regular colour tone. And of course, permanent hair removal is included as part of the package, although many of my clients don't require that, as you might imagine...You'll find, Claire," he said, leaning forward conspiratorially, "that there's very little we can't do." Another disarming smile. "Would you like a biscuit?"

When they left an hour later, she realised that no-one had mentioned the baby, not even once. She draped her arm guiltily over the emerging curve of her stomach, the little fish flips within demanding her renewed attention.

*

Philip and the doctor peered at her over the screen, their faces obscured by surgical masks. Philip gave her a thumbs-up.

"All OK?" asked the doctor, without waiting for an answer.

"You're doing great, baby," said Philip.

Philip and the doctor were now shining a light onto the area of interest, and Claire could hear them discussing what was to be done. Her and Philip, as a modern, right-on couple, had talked about this at length and had agreed that they would just ask for things to be kept as they were, with fixing any injuries being the main focus. Following the letter of the law, women technically had no say in what went on during a remodelling, but Claire was confident that Philip had her best interests at heart—he'd even paid the extra fee to allow her to remain awake for the procedure despite this being far from the done thing. They'd had to read between the lines, but the doctor had implied that it would be a collaborative process. Claire could hear the smiles in their voices as they spoke to her, an earnest attempt to reassure. But when she scanned their eyes they were blank; four pale orbs hovering coldly over the top of surgical masks. Knife-grey, shark-blue.

"So obviously, you can fix this, um...bit," she heard Philip mumble.

"I do think there's scope to go significantly tighter there, though, don't you agree?" mused the doctor. "Although, you do have to consider whether or not it would be comfortable."

For whom? She thought of the beetle again, and decided to have some gas and air, which was helpfully being proffered by a featureless nurse despite the anaesthetic rendering it superfluous. As she floated away on the comforting waves of nitrous oxide, she hoped that the baby was being looked after properly. Philip, while of course totally supportive, had drawn the line at breastfeeding. She closed her eyes and imagined shiny black armour and a pair of vicious pincers.

"We're just going to give your labia a little trim here, Claire," announced the doctor.

"What?" she croaked, trying and failing to sit up. "I don't want—"

"*The beetle's repeated attempts to right itself are ultimately fruitless*," said the narrator, "*and in the scorching sun, it is unlikely to survive.*"

Claire felt the sharp sting of a needle sliding into her upper arm. She tried to make her shell as hard as possible but too much of her soft underbelly was exposed for it to have any meaningful effect. All she could do was flail her arms, which seemed oddly dark and hairy under the bright lights. The last thing she heard before losing consciousness was the doctor apologising to Philip.

Together We Grow

My boyfriend is a plant enthusiast: the more exotic the better. Old man's beard, elk horn, fishbone. The bedroom is particularly full of them. They hang from curtain poles, draping down like Rapunzel's hair. Distressingly phallic cacti loiter in corners; succulents take up space where they shouldn't.

"Cacti are a type of succulent", he tells me.

"Whatever," I reply.

"You're succulent," he says, and bites my neck.

I go along with it, because it's easier.

When I get back from work more seem to have appeared.

"Did you buy more plants?"

"No," he says, flipping through channels. I squint at each wall, the table, the windowsill, unconvinced.

The other day, practically cooing, he'd showed me a timelapse of plants moving over a twenty-four-hour period, wiggling their little arms wherever the sun went. Disney versions of plants. Cute. Not like the ones in here, which seem to writhe and moan during the night, creeping tendrils into my dreams. When I wake up they're in different positions to when I went to sleep.

"Are you fucking with me?" I ask.

"What? No," my boyfriend replies.

"I wasn't talking to you."

The next week I'm reaching into the bookshelf when one of the cacti stabs me. That's the only way I can describe it: it skids along the shelf and plants its spiny arm into mine, deliberately. My boyfriend is coldly incredulous, the way he tends to be when anything unusual happens, as if the unknown is personally offensive to him. He said that I must have slipped when I was getting the book and was I on my period or something?

The paramedic said she'd never seen an allergic reaction like it.

I call in sick for the rest of the week, burrowing under the duvet and then abruptly emerging again as I come into contact with something lumpy and unexpected. I pull a fat little succulent out from down near my feet. Soil scatters over my arm, which has started to turn green.

When I wake up, more of them are in bed with me. My boyfriend has started to believe me, because last night he rolled over onto a cactus and now he's on the sofa, sulking. I keep trying to move them out, but as soon as I turn my back they've jumped in again, snuggling in close and giving happy little sighs. The swelling has started to go down, but my arm is green from shoulder to wrist, and soft spines have started to grow from where the little hairs used to be.

The next time I wake the old man's beard has moved from the curtain rail and is now perched directly above me. A seaweedy frond snakes around my wrist and grips iron-tight.

"Get off me!" I shout, struggling.

I think I hear it say *no*.

My boyfriend left a few days ago.

"Those plants are taking over your life," he said.

"I know," I said. "Sorry."

I haven't been able to move from the bed for several weeks now. More plants have gathered around, eager to join the fun. Each limb is bound with strong vines; my body tapestried to the mattress and woven over with flowers. Kindly souls drip nectar into my open mouth and allow me sips of water; I am leaf-skeleton light, but alive. My spines have hardened into dangerous points. I no longer know where the plants end and I begin.

Together, we begin to creep back to the perimeter of the room, to breathe and grow.

Waiting for the next one to join us.

In memory of Gauraa Shekhar, who edited this piece with kindness and generosity when it was first published at X-R-A-Y. 1995-2022

I Wanted to be Close to You

So I went to the forest. I breathed in the smell of pine that mingled with the sharp tang of earth. I ran my hands over the rough bark of the trees and felt the grooves, counting each one the way I used to run my finger over your ribcage as I explored the peaks and valleys of your flesh. I stood column-still to listen to the birds and the hushed rustle of the trees high above my head.

But it wasn't enough.

So I sat down on the forest floor. I explored the soft down of moss over rocks, acid-green velvet moist against my skin. I wove ivy into the dragging knots of my hair that you used to coil around your wrists at night. I marvelled at the spotted toadstools nestled in the undergrowth with their red-and-white promises of fairytale, just as dangerous and enticing as you were.

But it wasn't enough.

So I lay down in the undergrowth. I pressed my cheek against the ground and felt the damp crumble of soil beneath my fingertips. I watched as blind, pink worms squirmed their way to the surface and burrowed down again, while ants marched single file past my nose. I smelt the dank rot of a thousand dead things and inhaled it right to the bottom of my lungs. I felt closer to you.

But it wasn't enough.

So I started to dig. I clawed my eager hands into the dirt and kept on scrabbling, fighting down nausea as my fingernails bent back. I felt sweat roll in fat drops down my temples before being stopped in its tracks by the whispered breeze. I clutched my chest at the wild animal throb of my heart and the laboured rasp of my breath. I lay back and wrapped your arms tight around me, your cold bones finally resting against mine.

I Wanted to be Close to You

Grave Goods

Rachel's first date with Edward took place at the museum. She had opted for something sedate; she'd only just got back on the horse, after all, and she didn't want to find herself in a scenario she couldn't control. Edward had been agreeable, accompanying her around an exhibit about Anglo-Saxon England and cheerfully watching her consume an overpriced slice of lemon drizzle cake in a way that didn't make her feel pressured. She'd told him a little about what had happened—only the basics, but enough for him to know that she needed to be held at arms' length. She'd marked out clear boundaries, just as her therapist had suggested. The white band where her wedding ring once was had faded now, but her finger still pinched in at the bottom from where the metal had clung to her flesh.

After the cake, they spent a few minutes browsing the gift shop where Rachel noticed a section dedicated to the exhibit they'd just visited. She resolved to buy something as a memento, perhaps a comedy fridge magnet that she could wryly nod towards if things went awry, a manifestation of the extent to which she'd moved on with her life. Instead, she was drawn to a postcard of an elaborate pot, dotted all over with indentations. She turned it over to read the description.

Clay pot recovered from the Steadmere Anglo-Saxon Cemetery, York. Urns such as these were typically hand-made, and often decorated with various motifs. These included bosses, stamps and linear incised marks, as well as freehand designs.

There were small ceramic versions of the pots available to buy and, after weighing one in her palm for a moment, she marched to the till. Edward smiled at the purchase and the date was concluded with a tentative peck on the cheek and a promise to meet again. Once home, Rachel took her medication and completed her daily affirmations. *I did everything that I could.* She placed the pot on the bedside table next to the small, nondescript box that contained Mark.

Edward continued to message with cautious enthusiasm over the next few days, and when he suggested the museum again—*You seemed to enjoy it so much*—Rachel accepted. The Anglo-Saxon exhibition was still on so she made a point of locating the real-life version of the urn she'd somehow missed the first time. It was several times larger than the replica. Up close she could see fingerprints baked dry, the rough-but-deliberate carvings; the thousands of years of history that sang from its mottled surface. Her breath misted the glass of the display case as she leaned in to read the information plaque.

The Early Anglo-Saxon Period is characterised archaeologically by the regular deposition of artefacts in human graves in England. These artefacts are typically known as grave goods. It was believed that these offerings would accompany the deceased on their journey to another life, or be of use to them when they arrived there.

"What are you looking at?" Edward appeared at her shoulder, provoking a tiny flare of annoyance at the intrusion.

"Grave goods," she replied, as if she'd always known. At the gift shop she bought a second pot while Edward was in the toilet.

The date ended with a slightly more probing kiss and Rachel's subsequent declining of Edward's offer to go for a walk in the park. She felt distracted, nerves fizzing beneath her skin. When she got home she opened her laptop and typed in *grave goods.*

Some vessels found in graves were used as cremation urns, but in certain locations whole sets have been found, reminiscent of a table setting. This hints at a life well-lived, and the notion that rather than being consumed by flames, the deceased can instead participate in a banquet.

Rachel went upstairs and set down the new pot on the other side of Mark's box. Her phone buzzed. *I had a really nice time today*. She wondered if two pots was enough, then chided herself: hardly. She couldn't believe how stupid she'd been not to see it. He'd had nothing with him when he died, none of the luxuries that a long, drawn-out illness would have given him. He wasn't dressed in his favourite pyjamas, or clutching a photograph that meant something to him. He hadn't chosen just the right music for his funeral, because he was twenty-eight, for fuck's sake, and it would never have occurred to him to consider it. Mark was gone, just like that: too broken for a burial. Otherwise Rachel would have secretly tucked his Arsenal season ticket into his shroud and laid fresh lilies on his grave. All that was left of him was here, in the dull little box that hummed with energy and followed her everywhere she went.

She recoiled from the sudden flash of blue, sirens clamouring in her ears. The lights glowed behind her eyes for a while and she let them subside before scrabbling for her medication. She slept in fitful snatches and dreamt that she was curled inside a giant pot with Mark's ashes settling on top of her like grey snow, steadily filling her mouth until she choked herself awake.

The next morning, dressed in the clothes she'd slept in, Rachel went straight to the museum: it seemed like the right thing to do.

"Sorry, love. You can't come in."

Rachel blinked, the contents of her head shifting and reshaping themselves. "Excuse me?"

"Doesn't open 'til eleven." The security guard tapped the metal sign at the entrance.

"Oh! Oh, yes." Rachel understood now. The man peered at her as if he was going to say something else, then seemed to decide against it. It was only then that she realised it was raining, and her thin summer dress had gone see-through, clinging to her goosebumped flesh that glowed pale blue in the early morning light.

After four hours spent consuming pastries and jiggling her crossed legs up and down, Rachel spilled into the museum, mouth dry and fluttering with oily crumbs that made her teeth itch. She made her way to the Anglo-Saxon exhibition and stepped beyond the red cordon. A teenager with a shiny name badge that proclaimed him to be Jared appeared at Rachel's side, close enough for the chemical tang of his deodorant to invade her nostrils.

"Is there anything you'd like to know?" he asked.

"Oh, yes," replied Rachel, oddly touched by the livid constellations of acne blooming across Jared's tender cheeks. "Tell me everything."

Afterwards, in the gift shop, Rachel browsed the paraphernalia relating to the Anglo-Saxon exhibit but was at a loss; she'd already bought two pot replicas and there wasn't anything else appropriate; a plastic pencil sharpener or a jar of Ye Olde damson jam would hardly be fitting. Antsy and dissatisfied, she left the building and meandered along the street, occasionally smacking into pedestrians. She could, she supposed, make some sort of collection of all of his favourite things. Put them under a tree in one of the places he'd been happy. But the idea of his jaunty red football shirts and childhood stuffed tiger left sodden and decaying under clods of earth shot nausea through her. Her phone vibrated. *Is everything OK?* Angrily, she swatted the notification away.

*

Her shoulders heaved as she curled into the nondescript armchair, clawing at the box of tissues with the hand that wasn't encased in a plaster cast. Across the room, a blank-faced woman sat and nodded.

"I just... it was me who suggested going away. I *badgered* him. He'd just wanted to stay at home and I said he couldn't do that for his birthday, it wouldn't be special enough. So we went to York. We went and it was great. And then on the way back... I don't even know what happened. I was hungover so I was in the back seat with a pillow and—"

Fresh tears spilled out. The woman nodded.

"Take your time," she said. "It's still very early days. You're doing really well."

Rachel convulsed, somewhere between mortification at falling apart so comprehensively in front of someone she barely knew, and relief that at least someone was standing firm against the force of her grief, like no one else in her life had been able to.

"If I'd've been in the front seat…I'd be dead too." She was unable to clearly remember the rest, let alone articulate it, but isolated images ballooned in and out of her memory. The shocking power of the impact. How easily the car had crumpled, like tissue paper. Being outside the car, clawing at the mangled lump of the driver's door. How dark and sticky the blood became. Trying to perform CPR until she realised her arm was broken. And the lights. Always the lights. The aggressive blue flash of the emergency vehicles, the uniform glow of the cars behind all backed up because of the mess she and Mark had made, and the stars, blinking down pale and solemn as they waited for another soul to join them.

"Rachel. Rachel?" She became aware of the therapist leaning towards her. "I want you to know that what happened wasn't your fault. It was an accident."

Rachel shook her head. "But I didn't save him."

The therapist's eyes were calm and penetrating.

"Rachel. You did everything that you could."

In bed, mulling over the latest trip to the museum, Rachel realised where she'd been going wrong. She'd known that the replica pots were never going to be enough, that something else would be required. But now she understood that it was the real thing she needed: a complete set. A weighty and precious gift, sent belatedly into the afterlife so Mark wouldn't be alone. Something to atone for what she'd forced him to do, what she hadn't been able to do. *I'm sorry. I'm sorry.* She skipped her affirmations, and her medication too. It was getting in the way.

Rachel woke early. She put on her favourite dress and some lipstick—the magenta one Mark had always said made her look famous. She walked quickly to the museum; no issue with being admitted this time on account of it being a weekday. It was quiet. She made her way reverentially towards the Anglo-Saxon exhibit in the manner of a bride heading to the altar, slipping under the cordon with rehearsed grace. She took the hammer out of her rucksack.

It seemed to happen in slow motion. She felt nothing, heard only the tidal suck of her heartbeat roaring in her ears. She watched the glass cave in as easily as if it were made of spun sugar, observed the cuts that opened on her hands and wrists; the blood that flowed so emphatically someone else's concern. All against the backdrop of flashing lights, white and red, white and red, punching black dots in her vision as she tried to focus on the task at hand. She reached into the shattered display case and, for the first time, laid hands on the pot, dark smears of blood blemishing its surface. And wasn't that fitting, really, Rachel thought, from somewhere far away. She shifted her weight and braced herself as she removed the pot from its plinth.

Stop!

Put the item down, Miss!

At first she thought the voice was in her own head but the hand on her shoulder helped her to understand that it wasn't. Turning around, it was as if a dam had burst; every tuned out sense came thundering back and Rachel's head was a metal bowl ringing with the rhythmic blare of the alarms, the muffled static of the security guard's radio, the faraway whine of sirens, the incredulous chatter of tourists, the rasp of her own breath, the pain in her hands, the grinding crunch of glass beneath her sandals, the warm, wet, metallic-smelling mess of her blood slipping down the sides of the pot which was so heavy, heavier than she ever could have imagined. The lights went white and red, white and red, white and red, then blue blue blue blue blue blueblueblueblueblueblue until she was flat out on the tarmac looking up at the stars. The pot slid from her arms and shattered into oblivion, priceless shards of history incomprehensibly mingled with glass and blood and dust and clay and tears. As two police officers burst around the corner, Rachel closed her eyes. She had done everything that she could.

When She Laid an Egg

When she laid an egg it felt natural, as if she'd been born to do it. It slipped out with only a little discomfort and light mucus. After cleaning it up, she placed the egg on a small pillow she'd been saving for this exact occasion: blue velvet. She stroked its grainy shell. It was a pale cream colour, and warm to the touch. She fancied she could feel the life pulsate beneath its hard surface, although she knew that it was far too early for that. She posted a picture of the scene on social media, and watched the likes gush in.

She rolled the egg around in a designer buggy she'd bought on special offer, and tucked her charge in cosy under a hand-knitted yellow blanket with a satin trim. Passers-by oohed and aahed, offered unhelpful advice. She batted away their suggestions on sleep training and behaviour management with exasperated delight. She was proud of her egg. It made her feel complete, like a real woman, as if she'd finally found what she was looking for, and many other clichés.

Her friends threw her an egg party, as was customary. They played games like 'Guess the Circumference' and 'Pin the Yolk on the Egg'. She received gift after gift, endless tiny cushions of the softest silk, the lightest chiffon. They ate cupcakes with 'Hatching soon!' emblazoned across the fluffy butter icing.

It was nearly time. She wheeled the egg along slowly, an aching heaviness twisting her guts; her breathing laboured. She was excited to meet her little one, but almost fearful at it starting to belong to the rest of the world. Distracted by the bubbling pan of her thoughts, she tripped over a loose paving slab.

The egg bounced once, twice; leapt from its woollen trappings in a solemn, graceful arc. Time froze on the descent.

The egg made its final impact with the floor. Her stomach lurched; the world warped. When her vision had cleared she saw that somehow, miraculously, the egg remained whole. But as she lunged towards it a man with heavy boots blundered into its path. In one single step it was over. Miniscule fragments of shell gritted the pavement; clean and dry, like old bones.

On her knees, she scrabbled among the tiny porcelain pieces, searching for a drop of yolk, a soft centre—anything to prove that it hadn't been totally hollow all along. Against the tide of her fingertips, the dust of her egg began to sift and spread gently across the pavement, like sand sucked back into the ocean.

Shell Tide

There's terrible erosion down at Ballygort beach; the lumps clawed out of the cliffside make Mirabelle feel wasted just looking at them. There used to be a fine walkway up top, little steps down. Now it's just a peaty, slide-on-your-arse scramble to the shore: a death trap for anyone with weak ankles. Nonetheless, Mirabelle persists with her daily pilgrimage.

She picks her way over to the far side of the strand, ever the optimist when it comes to the search. When she'd first arrived, she'd entertained grand notions of setting up a beachcombing account on Twitter, but her romantic vision of coastal living has since diminished. It has to be said: nothing nice ever washes up here. Once, there was a dead dolphin that lay rotting for weeks, side carved open; miniature pin teeth bared in an eternal grimace. Mirabelle's instinct tells her there'd not be much of a market for pictures of that sort of thing. As it is, there are only so many people who'll retweet a piece of old bladderwrack. She scrolls through some of the established combers' blue-ticked accounts with increasing incredulity, their timelines resplendent with delicate fragments of sea glass and shells of implausible perfection. *Their* beaches, it seems, are like sodding gift shops.

Today, something is different. Instead of bare, tidemarked sands patterned by the ghosts of old waves, shells crunch underfoot, increasing in quantity the further she edges towards the rock pools. A ludicrous flip-flop of excitement jolts through her stomach and she almost breaks into a run, before hunkering down in a likely-looking area. Her hand is about to close around a perfect cockle shell when a shadow falls across her path, momentarily blocking out the light.

"We called it a shell tide when I was small."

The man has appeared out of nowhere: hands stuffed into pockets of a brown jacket, three-day-old stubble on his jaw. Average-looking, although they say that murderers and rapists often are. He smiles in a non-threatening sort of way.

"Sorry, I didn't mean to give you a fright. Just here for a walk."

It's exactly, Mirabelle thinks, the sort of thing a murderer or rapist *would* say. She reluctantly pulls herself up to standing and takes a step back, covertly slipping a sharpish-looking stone into her pocket. What she needs is a dog, preferably a large one.

As if summoned by a higher power, one appears. It's a huge, sandy-coloured lurcher, with a great pink rasher of a tongue that lolls out over surprisingly white teeth. Mirabelle extends an arm to pat its quivering haunch, as if taking decisive ownership will get the dog onside.

"Who do you belong to, then?" she asks the dog, although if she thinks about it, she might well ask the same thing of the man. It was something to say more than anything else, but now the question has left her mouth she's curious about the answer; pertaining to the dog, that is. Both she and her human companion peer down the empty beach, the man shading his eyes with his hand.

"It's the head of the one I had when I was young," he says. "He was called Banjo. Great fella; got hit by a car. I'm John, by the way." Mirabelle supplies her own name with enthusiasm, such is her relief that she won't be expected to formulate a response to the dead dog anecdote. There seems to be a cultural predilection here for sharing stories about death, but she's never had much of an appetite for it. The present-day dog, very much alive, is gambolling in huge circles and running after gulls with simple, muscular joy.

"It doesn't seem to have anyone with it," says Mirabelle. A small snarl of worry begins to swirl in the centre of her chest. She wonders if John feels the same, given his previous experience of dog ownership.

"We ought to catch it, I suppose," he says, confirming Mirabelle's hypothesis. They begin to walk towards the dog, falling into step beside one another. John smells faintly of cigarettes and Mirabelle is suddenly acutely aware of his adjacent physicality, the sleeve of his jacket brushing against hers. The dog, sensing capture, raises its head. Mirabelle knows this dance from dogs of her childhood: the key is to feign nonchalance, as if you just happen to be wandering over, and then grab them at the last minute. This dog, however, appears inconveniently astute. As soon as they set foot within a ten-metre radius it takes off, bounding up the sandbanks and into a nearby field that leads over the hill. Mirabelle turns to look at John, who returns her gaze. An unspoken decision is made.

The ground is boggy underfoot after a week of solid rainfall, and for a while the sound of squelching is all that punctuates the silence as they struggle up the incline.

"I'm sorry about your dog, by the way," offers Mirabelle—generously, she thinks—but John is too preoccupied with the state of his shoes to hear.

As they near the top, they stop to catch their breath and admire the view. A gust of wind whips up coat, scarf, hair, and Mirabelle suddenly feels as if she's on holiday, that this is what having an adventure might be like, and says as much.

"Your accent, you're not from here," says John. Mirabelle agrees that she isn't. John laughs, a short *ha*. "You know, it's customary to answer that question by telling me where you're from."

Mirabelle mulls this over. "Does it matter?"

John looks chastened.

"I suppose not," he concedes, kicking at a tuft of grass.

"Paris," says Mirabelle, relenting. "Well, from the suburbs. But my father is Irish."

"I used to live in France," says John, which seems convenient. Mirabelle wonders if he is a compulsive liar.

Before she can contemplate this further the dog makes itself heard; it sounds too far away altogether. They jump guiltily and make their way over the peak of the hill. As they stumble down the other side, Mirabelle spots the dog's tail disappearing over a wall in the distance, a yellow flag gliding over moss and stone.

Then a gunshot rings out, a crack that echoes horribly.

They're running now, impeded by the uneven ground. A gush of cold water trickles into Mirabelle's ankle boot. The wind has picked up, and a sharp bark whips through it.

John gets there first. "Jesus."

Mirabelle catches up, breathing hard, to discover the source of John's concern. The dog dips its head over the ravaged carcass of a sheep, mouth stained crimson and smiling. It wags its tail to see them.

"Ah, Jesus," John repeats. "I know the farmer whose fields these are. He's desperate for shooting things; he'd shoot a mouse for the craic." John is agitated, paces. "It's what did for poor Banjo in the end."

Mirabelle stops looking at the dog and the dead sheep.

"I thought he got hit by a car?"

John exhales, hands on his hips.

"Ah he did, sure, but that wasn't what killed him. He had to have an artificial leg for a while, but then he learned to run good enough without it. No, it was Donovan and his fecking rifle." He looks distressed. Mirabelle glances over her shoulder; the wind is swirling so much she can hardly hear and a fine drizzle has started to mist her eyelashes, obscuring her vision.

"We'd better move the dog, so." She fumbles in her pockets, fingers grazing against the sharp stone that she might still put to use yet, and takes out a scarf. It's a good silk one, pink and yellow, and she tries not to dwell upon how much it had cost as she approaches the dog who is panting now, tired from its exploits. She murmurs soothingly into its ear as she slips the scarf around its neck, turning it into a makeshift lead. As she gently guides the dog back over to John, she wonders if this is how she'll gain traction on Twitter. She imagines her lost dog post being shared over and over, connecting concerned animal lovers in far-flung destinations, all willing this troublesome creature back home. John reaches down to pat it and turns to Mirabelle, half-smiling.

"I don't suppose—"

Another gunshot snaps through the air and they both duck, Mirabelle dragging the dog down with her, eliciting a surprisingly piteous yelp. She slips and hits the ground hard, feels her teeth grind against her lip. John, on his knees, hauls her to hers. The dog clambers to its feet and shakes, splattering them both with mud and blood and God knows what else. Someone she can only assume is Donovan stomps into view, rifle smoking. A dead pheasant dangles from his fist. John staggers up and presses himself in front of Mirabelle and the dog.

"I'm warning you, Donovan, don't shoot!"

The dog strains against the leash, whimpering. Donovan takes another couple of steps forward to inspect the sheep. John shifts from foot to foot.

"I'll fight you, Donovan!"

The old man raises his head as if he's only just noticed them.

"What in the name of feck are you talking about?"

"Just leave the dog alone!" John's voice wobbles. Mirabelle lays a steady hand across his shoulder, as if he were a frightened horse. Donovan bundles the pheasant under his arm, gore smearing his anorak.

"That there," he says, gesturing with his free hand, "is my dog. And that sheep's been dead since morning, 'twas a fox that got her. You bloody eejit," he adds, under his breath. Mirabelle feels the scarf unspool from her hand as she slackens her grip and the dog trots meekly over to Donovan, seventy euros worth of silk trailing through the mud behind it.

They walk back to the beach with the sound of the waves filling the space between them, Mirabelle wondering how far afield she'll have to take her coat to be dry-cleaned in order to avoid people gossiping about her in the local supermarket.

The tide is almost in now, the carpet of shells sucked back into the foam. Mirabelle feels the breath catch in her chest, embarrassed at the strength of her disappointment.

"Oh." Her voice comes out small, like a child's. John is distracted, bending to pick something up.

"Ah, look," he says. It's an oyster shell, large and craggy with an undulating lip, porcelain-smooth on the inside. He holds it out to Mirabelle. "You could use it as a soap dish."

Mirabelle is momentarily flummoxed at the mention of soap dishes, and rearranges her thoughts rapidly to accommodate this new piece of insight into John, like one of those puzzles with sliding plastic tiles you'd find in a Christmas cracker. She starts to pocket the shell but changes her mind, giddy with a sudden rush of good feeling.

"No, you have it." She watches as John's ruddy cheeks pinken further and feels her own do the same.

As the shell changes hands, damp sand smears across both of their palms; a transaction that somehow feels as though a promise has been made. John clears his throat, jingles the change in his pockets.

"Suppose I'd better be going, then."

"Yes."

Mirabelle watches John walk back down the beach until he's nothing more than a speck on the horizon. She tosses the sharp stone from earlier into a rock pool where it sinks, quickly obscured by the dark, shifting sand. She licks her lips, tastes salt and blood. Closes her eyes and imagines the oyster shell cradling a fat cake of soap that'll whittle away a little more each day until there's nothing left at all.

All the Dead Girls

Nadine had unfinished business with the Northern Lights. She and Jason had chosen Norway for their honeymoon and booked the customary nighttime tour, seduced by the high-contrast, neon-tinted images on the company website that seemed to promise something profound and life-changing. They'd travelled out to the Tromsø countryside on a coach in the middle of the night, full of naïve anticipation at the thought of another thing to tick off their bucket lists. Outside, the wind whipped their cheeks raw as they stood shivering under the silence of the stars, waiting. The lights stubbornly refused to manifest.

"I think that's one there," the tour guide had said, pointing at a cloud.

Back at the hotel they'd inhaled grilled cheese sandwiches made by the kindly receptionist on night duty and fallen into bed, too exhausted to consider peeling off their double layers of thermal underwear in order to do what you're supposed to on a honeymoon. After three nights of this they admitted defeat and half-heartedly went clubbing in a place where one beer cost the equivalent of £25 and the music made them feel old.

Ten years later they were back in the Arctic Circle, or thereabouts, for their anniversary. They'd settled on Reykjavík, another place to chase the lights.

Nadine had read somewhere that Reykjavík was one of the safest cities you could visit, that sometimes there were entire years that passed without any homicides. The previous year there had been only one murder, the article had said, a twenty-year-old girl. A woman, technically, but she'd looked very young to Nadine. *Only one.* The words pounded her head in time with her feet on the pavement: *only, only, only*. She thought back to the image of the girl's smiling face staring out of her computer screen, the brightness in her eyes.

"Hello? Have I lost you?"

Nadine blinked at Jason's gloved hand waving in front of her face.

"Sorry." She consulted her guidebook. "Where are we heading to next?"

After half an hour spent taking careful photographs of the graceful swoop of the Hallgrimskirkja Cathedral, Nadine and Jason went for dinner at a pleasant fish restaurant. They were eating early in preparation for what they hoped would be *the* outing that evening, the one where they would finally see the lights.

"Nice, isn't it?" said Jason, as their plates were put in front of them.

"Mm." Nadine's food had come with some sort of redcurrant sauce which pooled stickily around the fish; she mustn't have been paying attention when she ordered.

"I can't stop thinking about that girl," she said.

"Which?"

"The one who was killed here last year, the one from the article."

"Oh, right." Jason frowned as he speared an asparagus tip with his fork. "Why her, and not anyone else?"

"Sorry?"

"Well, think of how many murders there are in somewhere like the UK each year, or even just in Dublin. I'd say one murder isn't really bad going, on balance."

Jason's relentless logic in the face of any sort of emotion often rendered Nadine temporarily inarticulate; his tendency to perceive everything through the lens of probabilities and averages. She tried again.

"It's just, it's so rare here. So it must have been particularly shocking for the community—"

"No, I get that," said Jason, waving his hand. "But objectively, there's no need to get bogged down in this one, is there? Especially when you think about how safe it is here, *in general*."

Nadine watched Jason as he chewed his monkfish, cheeks working hard, almost excessively, to break down the rubbery mouthful. The way he held his knife and fork drew attention to how large his knuckles were. She looked down at her own plate, the slab of dead fish in the shining red sauce, and took a sip of her wine.

"But don't you think," she persisted, "that the fact that she'd have felt safe makes it even sadder? She'd have thought she was OK, and then it was just… ripped away from her. And her family—"

Nadine could feel herself getting upset; the crack in her voice and the pain in her chest. The people at the table next to them were looking. She couldn't explain why this particular case had gotten to her so much; Jason wasn't wrong, after all. There was a Twitter account she grimly followed that documented every woman killed during the year to date, stacking up the figures week on week. A scrollable Who's Who of all the dead girls. Impotence made her belligerent. "Don't you think it's sad?"

Jason reached across the table to cover her hand with his.

"Of course I do." He left a respectable amount of time. "Will we ask to see the dessert menu?"

It was reported that the girl had got in someone's car, looking for a lift home. That wasn't something Nadine herself would ever do, not that she was victim blaming, it's just that it was different in other cities. Maybe that's why this was so upsetting: it was nice to think of *only one* woman somewhere, anywhere, feeling safe enough to wander down the street at night. The girl's murder demonstrated that this was clearly too much to ask, wherever you were. Perhaps this was why Jason's reaction bothered her so: the realisation that he just didn't understand; that he never really would.

There was an incident in her early twenties, living in London, when a messy night out culminated in a lost bank card and a dead battery, and she had to walk home. Spurred on by necessity and an emboldening cloak of fruit cider she set off, tucking her bag tightly in beside her, looking over her shoulder every few paces.

It almost felt inevitable when it happened: the quickening footsteps on the other side of the road, then behind her. The hand on her shoulder, the scuffle, his oddly unfocused eyes. That she managed to twist away was nothing but pure luck. She ran chaotically, desperately, and it was only when she skidded into the brightly-lit doorway of a twenty-four hour Tesco that she let herself acknowledge the burning in her lungs and the very real possibility that she might vomit all over the worn carpet at the entrance.

Nadine stayed in Tesco for over an hour, waiting for the feeling in her chest to dissipate. A hangover was starting to kick in but she was strung out, shaky, as if her feet couldn't quite touch the ground. She whiled away at least twenty minutes in the houmous aisle, silently reciting all the different varieties to herself, running her fingertip over the colourful, uniform stacks. *Caramelised onion, lemon and coriander, reduced fat, roasted red pepper.* The staff probably thought she was on drugs.

By the time she dared leave it was light and she had sobered up. She hurried home and crawled into bed, never mentioning what had happened to her housemates. It wasn't the only close shave she'd had, of course it wasn't, but it was the one that had stuck with her the most.

After the debacle of the meal, Nadine decided not to go on the lights chasing trip that evening. She didn't say much to Jason about it, taking a strange, defiant pleasure in communicating her decision in clipped tones. Jason, in fairness to him, took it in his stride, occupying himself over the next few hours by reading a book about Vikings while twisting the foil from a KitKat wrapper into the shape of a tiny longboat. Nadine had been disappointed to find out that the traditional ten year anniversary gift was tin or aluminium, which struck her as a singularly unromantic choice. She wasn't sure how inspired you could expect people to be by a toaster, or staples. They hadn't bothered with it in any case. Nadine turned a page in the guidebook and tried not to let the sound of rustling foil burrow like worms into her brain.

Apparently, there were several different mythical interpretations of the Northern Lights, but one of the most persistent seemed to be that they were the souls of the dead. It was hit or miss as to whether this was considered to be a good or bad thing; whether you should hide away or open yourself up to convening with the deceased. Some people believed that if you looked at the lights, they would reach down and snatch you away. Nadine peered at the accompanying photograph and saw turquoise hair billowing; electric green arms reaching, grasping, fading. She snapped the book shut and left it on the bedside table.

The next morning, on a whim, Nadine booked a trip to the Blue Lagoon. Jason wouldn't come with her; he'd never liked water much, and he wanted to spend time looking at the antique shops downtown. This was fine, ideal, actually, because wasn't it healthier for couples not to be joined at the hip, to have their own interests? Nadine decided that it was, and popped her fleece on over her swimming costume.

On arrival at the Blue Lagoon she was given a rubber wristband that fastened with a buckle. It contained a fob you could use to order drinks at a swim-up bar, which seemed a tad excessive. Nonetheless, Nadine resolved to make the most of it and self-consciously ordered a milkshake made with some sort of Icelandic yoghurt, then retreated to an edge.

As she relaxed into the experience she started to enjoy herself: the warmth of the water contrasting with the chilled air on her face and shoulders; the fluorescent blue of the lagoon against the backdrop of black volcanic rock.

"Pretty cool, right?" The man had sidled up to her without her realising. He spoke with an accent that she couldn't quite place.

"Yes," she replied, noting that the man was considerably younger than her.

"I come here a lot," he said. "It's great." He stretched expansively to reveal a muscular stomach and wet tufts of golden hair in his armpits. Nadine could smell the faint tang of alcohol on his breath. She folded her arms over her chest, still grappling with the milkshake, and hoped that her wedding band was visible.

"It's my first time," she said, compelled to be polite, before panicking that this sounded semi-sexual. "I'm here for my wedding anniversary, actually." The guy grinned and made a show of looking around.

"Where's your husband?"

Nadine took a step away.

"He's in the toilet."

"Cool. Well, you have a good day now."

He waded off. Nadine watched him stop at the bar, where he exchanged words with a couple of other men. One of them laughed. Nadine wondered if talking to her had been a dare.

She half-swum, half-stumbled away, and found an area slightly separate from the most crowded part of the lagoon. As she sunk down so that only her face was exposed to the air she noticed deposits of grey-white mud congealing at the sides of the pool. This must be the silica that she'd read about in the guidebook, supposedly boasting quasi-magical healing properties for people with psoriasis. She experimented with putting some of it on her face. It smelt strongly of sulphur. She layered on more and more until her face was thickly coated, her hair too; smeared it over her whole body until she could barely see her skin. No one talked to her after that.

When she went to the changing rooms to shower she caught her reflection in the mirror, dried mud crisp and flaking around her startled eyes, hair hanging in crusty ropes. She didn't look like herself any more.

That evening Nadine felt ready for the light-chasing excursion; maybe the mud did have healing properties, after all. Instead of a formal dinner, she and Jason had fish and chips but the gourmet kind, where the chips were sprinkled with rosemary sprigs and large flakes of sea salt. While they ate they talked in resolute, non-controversial circles, both keen to avoid the tension of the previous evening.

The temperature had dropped significantly since yesterday and the exposed parts of Nadine's face stung as she made the short dash from the hotel onto the coach. As they travelled out into the countryside Nadine looked out of the window, but all she could see was darkness and her own reflection. It all felt very familiar to the last time, ten years ago, except that this time she was in no way certain they'd see what they wanted to.

It was around midnight when they came to a stop and were ushered out by the cheerful tour guide, who assured them that this was a famously good spot for a sighting. As they waited, blowing into their hands and stamping their feet, Nadine noticed a young couple, hand-clasped and leaning into one another. She found herself wondering if it was their honeymoon, or some other special occasion for them. Or maybe, she considered, they were simply in love. A gasp from the crowd drew her attention skywards.

"Here we go," said the guide.

The sky split into waves of green, blue, purple, then split and warped again, pulsating as far as Nadine's vision would stretch; there could be no question of looking away, she realised. The crows of pleasure from the gathered tourists somehow mingled perfectly with the undulating colours. Instinctively, Nadine reached for Jason's hand but he wasn't where she thought he was and she found herself clutching at air. She turned to find him and saw him standing apart from the rest of the group, tears glistening in his eyes, his expression something she'd never seen before. She looked again to make sure she wasn't imagining it, that it wasn't some irregularity caused by the changing light. Jason didn't cry: he just wasn't that sort of person. He hadn't even cried at his mother's funeral, remaining steadily dry-eyed right down to the very last drink at the wake.

The lights danced around them but Nadine now watched Jason and not the phenomenon she'd waited a decade for. As the colours moved over his face, green and turquoise and purple, it occurred to her that perhaps she didn't really know him at all.

Nadine felt her own tears come as she looked back up at the technicolour sweep of souls: all the dead girls swirling across the stars, fading away as quick as they'd appeared.

You Can't Kill it Because it's Already Dead

The place is fancy and you say so and they don't reply so you say it again and they say *what?* and you say *never mind* and so you wind a smile around your face to stop your guts falling out of your mouth and take a sip of the dark red drink you're handed with steam coming off the top and they sigh and look out of the window at the people walking down the street having a nice time and as the unfamiliar drink starts to burn in your chest you try to breathe deeply and end up choking and they pat you on the back without really touching you and then the smartly dressed person says *come this way* and so you do and when you step into the lift the light from your wedding ring winks in the mirror like it's mocking you and you touch your hand to the wall of the lift only to find that it's melted away and when you look down you see that your fingers are disintegrating too, skin dripping over metal like candle wax, then you close your eyes because it's too shiny in here, too bright and you suddenly don't know what it is that you were trying to achieve when you booked this but you suppose it's like when a butterfly comes out of its chrysalis wrong and its wings are crumpled and wasted and you know it's going to die a slow death and you really ought to put it out of its misery and squash it there and then but your sentimental nature is holding you back from delivering the killer blow because of how beautiful it could have been if things had only been different, if only you'd tried harder, and so you let it carry on trying to live, you let it suffer until one day you notice it's dead, finally dead: hopeless and flawed and crumbled into dust and you hadn't even realised.

Puff

Chris hadn't gone to work again today. Lin thought about this as she alternated between picking at a cereal bar and gnawing the slivers of skin around her thumbnail. It had been happening more and more lately; she'd got used to the cold, flat sheet beside her each morning, the tight feeling in her chest as she entered the lounge to find him curled in his usual place beneath the tartan blanket that she'd come to hate with a visceral intensity.

"No luck?" she'd venture. Sometimes, he wouldn't even acknowledge her. Mostly, he'd just shake his head with the sad confusion of a defective nodding dog, then retreat back into the blanket. She'd burn that fucking thing one day.

Chris had never been a big sleeper. Back when they'd first started going out, he'd stay up late, usually on his laptop or listening to music. It hadn't been a problem then; Lin would join in on weekends, a willing tourist in a nocturnal world of the offbeat films that came on at three in the morning and half-asleep sex as the dawn crept in. They'd wake at eleven and ooze into the day, cocooned in the cottony-soft certainty of togetherness. But they weren't twenty-three anymore, and Chris's night-time quirks had evolved into full-blown insomnia that had worsened to the extent that he barely functioned. All the housework fell to Lin now, all the mealtimes. All the school runs. And any time the kids randomly woke up in the night, Chris was too much of a wreck to deal with them.

Sometimes Lin would bite her knuckle very hard, until she could feel her teeth connect with the bone. At the risk of sounding melodramatic, she didn't know how long she could carry on like this, with her zombie husband choking the life out of their family and whittling her down to a small, hard lozenge of a person. Oh no, Chris wasn't depressed; he wouldn't consider medication, or seeing the doctor. He was too tired for sex, and laundry, and paying bills, and going out for lunch. He was too tired for marriage counselling, naturally.

It was after another particularly bad morning, where a listless Chris wouldn't acknowledge her or the children at all, and Ethan had asked in a piping voice: "Is Daddy going to die?" that Lin made a deal with herself. One month, she told herself. One month. If things hadn't improved by then, she was done. She didn't really see what could change in a month after things had been like this for so long, but she settled on the time limit to exonerate herself from the shittiness she felt when she thought about having to break it to the kids. She had no money spare, no secret running away fund; but if it came to it, they could probably move in with her mum. The thought of her mother's mouth puckering into its characteristic cat's arsehole of disappointment galvanised her into a manic frenzy of internet trawling, rattling through the usual suspects with depressing ease. Illegal sleeping pills from the U.S, sleep retreats, hypnosis. Jade eggs, melatonin, CBT. Divorce solicitors.

Lin spent her lunch hour that day ricocheting around the lifestyle section of a department store, accosted by women who tried to sell her perfume and made her want to kill things. The tinny notes of Christmas songs jangled her already popping nerves, particularly as it was only fucking November. She was about to leave, defeated, when she noticed a small display that was so tucked away she might have missed it. A modest pyramid of boxes sat behind three pale pink grubs, each about the size of a rabbit and emitting a cosy red glow. They were moving up and down as if they were breathing, and felt oddly warm and flesh-like to the touch. Lin had reached out to one of them, then snatched her hand away at the unnerving sensation that she was stroking a featureless baby. She studied one of the boxes.

PUFF—the robot who breathes with you!

It was a sleep robot, the blurb explained, whose breathing was designed to mirror and regulate your own. There were in-built carbon dioxide sensors that slowed your breathing down, resulting in deep relaxation. Despite its disconcerting appearance, Lin felt strangely soothed by the rise and fall of its smooth skin and its rhythmic, snuffled breaths, the seasonal chaos around her somehow less oppressive. How much was this thing? A quick rummage with the box revealed a price tag of £599, which was ludicrous, obviously. She spent a few moments totting up that month's finances, got the calculator on her phone out. It was far more than they could afford. But the spectre of Chris with his dead eyes and sour-smelling blanket was ever-present, and Lin's thoughts abruptly crystallised: she was going to put it on the credit card. It could be an early Christmas present for all of them, she reasoned. She felt almost festive as she made her way back to the office.

Once the kids were in bed, Lin went into the living room and dumped the box into Chris's lap. He explored it like a dementia patient trying to understand whether or not his hands belonged to him.

"Open it!" urged Lin, impatient and giddy with the fragile burst of optimism that she'd carried with her since lunchtime. She got the thing out of the box and turned it on, and it immediately snuffled into life, starting to rise and fall with little snores. “It’s called a Puff,” she laughed, slightly too loudly.

“Puff,” repeated Chris, the suggestion of a smile briefly altering his grey features.

“Yes,” said Lin, kneeling down so that her elbows rested on Chris’ lap. ‘To help you sleep. Can you give it a go, Chris? Please?’ He nodded, with what looked like some effort. Lin bit back her annoyance; his neck wasn’t fucking broken.

“I will. I’m just, so, you know—”

“Tired. I know. But you need to try. You need to—” Lin’s voice cracked, her brittle high spirits tipping over into the familiar sweep of panic. She pressed the bridge of her nose and breathed deeply. “I’m tired too.” This statement floated between them, hovering on Puff’s artificial breath.

“I can sleep in the spare room tonight,” offered Lin. “So you can see how you get on.” Chris nodded again, and they smiled a wavery truce at each other.

That night Lin went to sleep in the spare room with a strange feeling of anticipation reminiscent of Christmas Eves of her childhood, with a notable difference being that Santa was now in the form of a blind silicone grub, and she was relying on him to save her marriage.

The alarm went off at six and Lin stumbled to the living room out of habit. The tartan blanket was abandoned on the sofa, coiled and empty like a discarded snakeskin. Jarred, Lin ran to their bedroom where she found Chris curled under the duvet, one arm slung over the Puff. She found herself checking his breathing like she used to with the kids when they were tiny. *Was* he breathing? At first she could only hear Puff making its little wheezing sighs.

“Chris!” she shrieked, shaking his shoulders, ripping off the duvet. “Chris, wake—” Chris’s eyes flicked open and he shuddered, disorientated.

“I was… asleep.”

“You were. God. Sorry,” said Lin, attempting to master the adrenaline jangling through her chest. “How was it?”

“It was…good. Thing works.” He gestured vaguely towards the Puff, yawning. “I’m gonna…do you mind if I…?”

“No! No, no, go on. I’ll just…I’ll leave you to it.” Lin whispered. She shut the door and pressed her forehead hard against the frame before heading into the kitchen to get the kids’ breakfast ready, still trembling slightly.

When they returned home that evening, via work and after-school club, Chris was dressed, and looked like he’d showered. He hovered next to the kitchen counter.

"How was your day?" he offered. "I managed to get a few bits at the shop. You know, for dinner."

"Thanks." Lin pulled her coat off and reached for a wine glass in a single fluid motion. Charlie and Ethan flung themselves down in front of the TV, both turning to glance at Chris as if he were a mildly interesting exhibit at a museum, before returning their focus to the screen.

"I feel different," Chris said. "It's been so long since I've actually slept. It's..." he lifted his arms and flapped them down by his sides while Lin swallowed a gulp of rioja so quickly that it made a painful bubble in her throat.

"You look different. It's... I don't know what to say," she laughed. "This is weird." Chris took a tentative step towards her.

"I thought we could try...could we make dinner together?"

Lin chopped and diced while Chris nervously measured out pasta, soundtracked by the boys' giddy laughter at whatever they were watching. After dinner and a slightly stunned couple of hours in front of the TV, Chris had started to nod off. Lin returned from putting the boys to bed and watched him as his eyelids fluttered and he clutched a corner of the tartan blanket that was once again back on the scene after this morning's brief respite. She was swept back to when the boys were young and crashed out after a day playing outside, chubby faces crumpled and angelic as they grasped teddies and lost themselves in their dreams. A crash on the TV brought Chris juddering out of his slumber, drool glazing the corners of his mouth.

"Hey," said Lin. "Sleeping again!"

"Yeah. I think...I'm gonna go in...do you mind?"

"Not at all. Absolutely. Go! Have fun!" Lin was wildly overenthusiastic in her encouragement, ushering him into the bedroom in the manner of a parent waving off a socially awkward child to their first disco. She tucked him in, suppressing her pavlovian disgust of the blanket. Chris snuggled into the Puff and closed his eyes.

Days passed and Puff started to become a fixture in their lives. The boys had been 'introduced' to it and treated it like a pet. "Thank you for helping Daddy," she heard Ethan cooing to it one afternoon, Puff's rosy glow lighting up his little face.

If she had been prone to whimsy, Lin would have likened Chris's transformation to a butterfly emerging from a chrysalis; as it was, a knackered forty-something shrugging his way out of a mangy blanket was hardly the stuff of nature documentaries. Still, things were undeniably better than they'd been in months. She'd finally convinced Chris to visit the doctor and get signed off from work for a month, and he'd got into a gentle routine of buying groceries and starting the dinner prep for when she got in. After some tentative afternoons watching TV together, Chris had started taking the boys to their swimming lessons. They'd adjusted to his sudden re-entry into their lives with sunny, uncomplicated acceptance; Lin tried not to find this irritating. She spent her new-found free time taking long, luxurious baths, staring into the mirrored domes of bubbles until her eyes watered and she had to blink the hundreds of tiny reflected Lins away.

One evening, after the boys were in bed, Chris had gestured vaguely towards Lin's laptop.

"Why don't you have a look at some of those language courses you wanted to do. One of the evening ones."

Lin sat up.

"Really? Can you handle that? Dinners, bedtimes..."

"Yes," said Chris stoutly. "Just have a look." Lin pondered the novelty of spending an evening on her computer that didn't involve weighing the merits of a sleep retreat in Thailand against a course of hypnosis. Chris cleared his throat and spoke, his voice barely audible.

"It's just that I know that I've been holding you back."

Three weeks after Puff's arrival, Lin had booked a couple of days of annual leave to spend some time with Chris, and quite unexpectedly, they'd ended up having sex for the first time in over a year. It was faltering and awkward, both of them shy with each other; but as Chris reached out to her afterwards Lin understood that there was still something there; however small, however damaged. After that, Lin moved back into the main bedroom and they rediscovered spooning, albeit with Puff wedged between them.

The next day Chris had been difficult to wake, but was eventually roused with some spirited bashing from Ethan. After dropping the kids at school and a trip to the shops, they had a pleasant, uneventful lunch together, followed by a companionable couple of hours spent reading. When Lin left to do the after-school club pick-up, Chris was in the kitchen getting the dinner started.

On the way back, Lin put the radio on for the boys; the local station was playing Christmas songs and they all sang along and counted the trees in the windows on the high street. They were still laughing and singing when Lin put her key in the front door.

"Daddeeeeeeeee!" shouted Ethan, bowling through to the living room. "Oh. Daddy's asleep."

"What, poppet?" Lin shucked off her coat and hurried after him where she found that Chris was indeed asleep, a vision in tartan. An onion lay half-chopped on the kitchen counter with the knife laid out at an odd angle. She realised that Chris was very still. She dropped her handbag.

"Chris. Chris. Can you hear me, Chris?" Lin tapped Chris sharply on the shoulders the way you were taught to in first aid, swiftly progressing to a violent shake when his eyes didn't open. "Chris! Charlie, take Ethan upstairs." Charlie complied, ushering Ethan out with far too much composure for a seven-year-old. Lin found a weak pulse with shaking fingertips. She called an ambulance.

The front window lit up with the steady flash of fluorescent blue, which jarred horribly with the cheap multicoloured lights adorning the Christmas tree. Lin switched them off. The paramedics bustled in and took over with brisk professionalism.

"He's conscious, but his breathing and heart rate are far too slow," said the one who was clearly in charge. "Technically he's medically stable but we're going to have to take him in. Has there been anything out of the ordinary recently? Any new medication?" Lin shook her head.

"No, nothing. Although...he has been using a sleep aid, though. Do you think...?" she faltered as the two paramedics exchanged a look.

"Which one?" Lin dug Puff out from behind the cushions, still pulsing. That look between the paramedics again. "Yeah, that checks out," said the younger one. "I'd turn that off if I were you." Puff continued to wheeze and sigh, its red light suddenly a warning.

"I'm sorry?" The paramedics started to heft Chris onto a stretcher.

"We've seen a few of these recently. They're pushing for a global recall of these things but there's legal stuff in the way as the company won't have it. I tried to tweet about it but I got a warning and—"

"Saj." The older paramedic shook his head.

"All I'm saying, is have a look at the small print," muttered Saj, as they manoeuvred Chris into the ambulance. Lin pelted up the stairs to her wardrobe where she found the empty Puff box and its creased set of instructions. She scanned through, eyes blurring.

This iteration of the Puff model (AH231j) has been tested with a small sample of volunteers who all reported no serious side effects; however this study has not yet been peer-reviewed or repeated in significant numbers. As such NoctisTech accepts no liability for any adverse effects experienced by users of this device.

There was a number to call: no answer. She tried the website listed: *this domain name does not exist*. She went into the boys' bedroom where Charlie and Ethan were curled up in the bottom bunk. She got in too.

After a couple of nights in hospital it became clear that Chris wasn't coming home. He was in a coma, and the doctors were mystified. Charlie and Ethan slumped dazed in front of a saccharine marathon of Christmas films, while Lin knocked back wine and scoured internet forums with grim obsession.

There's no point in turning it off once they go unconscious, it's too late by then. Trust me, I know.

my wife has been asleep for 3 months now!!! we need justice

I can't believe this, I've got four children. My youngest isn't able to cope, he cries constantly.

I thought it would help.

Lin had tried to turn Puff off, but it had continued breathing, and still glowed red. She put it in a bin bag at the bottom of the wardrobe and moved back into the spare room.

On Christmas Eve, Lin went to bed and felt nothing, no anticipation bubbling in her stomach this time. She'd put on a brave face for the boys; made them hot chocolate, left things out for Santa. She downed the glass of sherry and curled up into the foetal position on top of the duvet.

The next morning, stiff and cold, Lin dragged herself up. In spite of—or perhaps because of—the fact that it was 8am, she poured herself a glass of brandy. She called up to Charlie and Ethan in a too-bright voice, laughter or tears in danger of spurting out.

Lin was impressed with how tall she'd managed to make the bonfire. She stood back, sweating despite the cold, and took another slug of brandy. The damp wood smoked and complained as the fire took hold, first caressing and then hungrily consuming the blanket that lay tucked among the branches. Charlie and Ethan whooped and capered, their visible breath punctuating the air in short bursts. Lin bit down on her knuckle until the frost at her feet glittered scarlet, and the blanket was nothing but ash.

TimeOut

Nap time. Jen put Mila in her cot and went to leave the room. Not quickly enough, as it turned out: Mila's face immediately crumpled into a scream. Jen scrabbled at her phone to locate the TimeOut app and with a couple of taps, set the baby to 'off'. Mila froze, arms mid-windmill, her rage suddenly impotent. Jen didn't like it when she was too slow to activate the app; it was disturbing returning to a tiny, anguished statue once TimeOut was over. Still, it was early days, and she'd get better with practice. That was parenthood, right?

Mila Rose Donaldson had arrived eight weeks ago, and she was just *perfect*. During TimeOut Jen would scroll through pictures of her, amazed that something so beautiful had been created by the splicing of her and Daniel's DNA. They'd opted for the Extra-Utero Gestative Capsule; fairly new technology—pioneering, in fact—but Daniel was lucky enough to have great private health insurance, and after weighing up all the pros and cons they'd decided to just *go* for it. To Jen, it seemed nothing short of insane that anyone would choose to go through pregnancy and childbirth when there were other, easier options. You didn't get a *medal* for giving birth in a field with no pain relief, for goodness sake, and why needlessly wreck your pelvic floor? Of course, she'd had to find a specialist antenatal group to attend: she would have felt too weird sitting there with no bump. She'd have felt, I don't know... judged. People could be a bit funny about that sort of thing.

"How will the baby feel without hearing your heartbeat, your voice?" demanded her friend Molly one afternoon as Mila was entering her sixth month of gestation. As she spoke, Molly stroked the head of her own ten-week-old, Caspar, currently suspended between her breasts by a stretchy cloth wrap that stank of sour milk.

Jen was enthusiastic. "They've thought of all that! They record everything so it can be played to the baby on a loop, so it doesn't know any different. It says that—"

"Yeah, you showed me the leaflet before," said Molly. "But it's not the same, surely?"

"They've been doing this for really premature babies for a while now, though, haven't they?" Jen countered. She didn't like it when Molly got like this. Caspar was her third; she co-slept with all of them at once and liked to broadcast the fact that she hadn't had a full night's sleep for the last five years as if it were something to be proud of.

Molly narrowed her eyes.

"But that's the thing, yours isn't premature, is she?" The silence that followed was interrupted by Caspar beginning to stir. A shiny pink nipple was duly produced and everything was quiet again save for the sound of the baby's contented sucking.

The EUGC package came with some amazing add-ons. You could obviously choose sex and eye-colour and things like that (female and blue), but there were *so* many other things included to make your life easier. They'd thought of everything! The best, in Jen's opinion, was the TimeOut feature. It was an app that enabled you to literally turn the baby off so they could get the sleep that was so crucial to their development. The exact right amount of sleep for each age range was calculated and all you had to do was follow the prompts from the app. Naturally, you had to sign the code of ethics and agree to visits from the research team; you weren't supposed to keep them off for *ages* or anything. You just ensured that they didn't get overtired and cranky. It was a total no brainer, although for obvious reasons she had decided not to mention that particular detail to Molly for the moment.

Jen's phone pinged with a notification from TimeOut: *What's nappening?* It was time to turn Mila back on. Jen did so when she was just outside the nursery door, so that when she entered the room Mila had already unfrozen from her rictus and broken into a gorgeous, dimpled beam.

*

16 weeks old now and Mila was just a *dream*. Hard work though, keeping her entertained! She had a touch of reflux, so she cried a lot and didn't like being put down. When are they going to make an app for that? thought Jen, wiping up sick for the fifth time that day. Jen loved Mila, so much, *obviously*, but there was only so much crying one could tolerate before becoming just a little frazzled. Daniel was super-supportive, but at the same time Jen wasn't sure he totally got it. He didn't get home from work until Mila was off for the night, so he'd just peep in at her in the nursery as she lay static and doll-like.

Looking after Mila when she was on was hard, harder than she'd thought it would be. It would be nice to just...you know. Have a break. Mila had been having her TimeOut for the last 45 minutes but Jen had spent the whole time doing laundry. Again. TimeOut pinged: *Nap's up!* Jen turned her phone over. Ten minutes more wouldn't hurt.

*

It was the day for the CapTots meet up, which was the baby group attached to the EUGC antenatal class. They met every month or so, and it was *so* nice to see how everyone was getting on. The café they were meeting at was slightly out of Jen's way so she'd kept Mila off for the car journey as the screaming would have been a *nightmare* otherwise. It wouldn't have been safe to drive, actually.

"How are you, darling?" trilled Kelly, as Jen jostled her buggy between the tables. "We've saved you a high chair!"

"Oh…thanks. We ate at home, actually."

The babies were all around nine months old at this stage, but Mila wasn't quite ready for solids yet. Jen was sure it was fine—babies' development wasn't totally linear, everyone knew that. She just preferred not to discuss it.

"How…is…MILA!" cooed Cassie. "Oh! She's so dinky still!"

Mila *did* seem very small compared to the other babies, but then, Jen herself was small. Cassie flaunted the large and cherubic Joshua on her knee, who squealed and clapped his hands, almost freakishly alert. "He's started to say 'Mama' already," she announced.

The familiar ping signalled the end of somebody's TimeOut—this time it was Ola and baby Lily. The whole group had unanimously opted for the app with their EUGC packages—they'd discussed it quite a lot during their antenatal classes and had all agreed that you'd be mad not to. Sleep deprivation was a form of torture, after all! Ola scrambled to turn Lily back on ("I just feel guilty if I leave her off even a second too long,") while everyone nodded in agreement.

"She'll be fine, surely?" said Jen. "A couple of minutes won't make a difference." The resulting appalled hush that settled like snow indicated the depth of Jen's *faux pas*.

Jesus, it wasn't as if she'd suggested daily acid baths.

"Leaving them off for longer than the recommended nap times can harm their development, they explained that at the classes," said Ola.

"What, do you leave Mila off for longer than the app says to?" Kelly tilted her head to one side.

Jen stood up, her chair grating backwards. "Do you know what, I forgot that we have a doctor's appointment. Been great catching up!"

Back in the car, Mila started to scream, and Jen switched her off without putting up a fight. She was about to turn the key in the ignition when her phone went: Molly. It was an email with a link to an article. *Have you seen this?*

It's fucking barbaric.

Widespread abuse of baby sleep app causing severe developmental delays, recent study finds.

Jen sat for a long time. She started to read.

*

Mila was crying. Wailing, in fact. Of course she was: it was 3am, she wasn't used to being up at this time. Nor was Jen. Jen shook a rattle as she gulped her coffee. *Shake shake shake. Twinkle twinkle. Let's stay awake.* Daniel came in for the third time that night, pulling out his earplugs.

"Jen, seriously? What the fuck are you playing at?"

Jen spoke slowly over the noise.

"I've already explained—I sent you the article. We need to *keep* her up so she can *catch* up."

"But you've both barely slept for three days now, this is ridiculous. You'll both be ill. Listen to her!" Daniel tried to pick Mila up as her screams escalated but Jen blocked him.

"We have an EUGC visit first thing tomorrow!" she shrieked. "We don't have time to sleep!"

Daniel shook his head.

"Jen...how long have you been leaving her turned off for?"

Round and round the garden, like a teddy bear. Come on sweetheart! Don't be sad.

Jen poured herself another coffee, and waited for the knock at the door.

First Time at the Allotment

At night I whisper the names of the forbidden: *Parsnip. Celeriac. Artichoke. Aubergine.* The words snap and crunch in my mouth, their defiant taste far sweeter than the ribbons of candy floss that swirl in my guts like long pink tapeworms.

Each morning, Mama stands over me as I force down chocolate ice cream with hot fudge sauce. I sneak a look out of the window toward the hills beyond the woods where the man keeps his allotment: I learnt about him from reading the newspaper the doughnuts come wrapped in. Mama found the grease-stained scrap underneath my pillow and wept anguished tears for the delinquent daughter who always wanted what she couldn't have.

Mama sends me to collect the weekly order of cupcakes from the bakery and I take the money but decide that today is the day I finally go beyond the woods. I've waited long enough. *Asparagus. Pumpkin. Cauliflower. Mushroom.* By the time I emerge from the thicket of trees I'm trembling from sugar withdrawal.

I fall against the shiny front door which opens to reveal the man from the doughnut paper, as if he were expecting me. He gestures for me to follow him; I don't wait to be asked twice. My vision blurs with tears as I take in the long-awaited allotment: a paradise so vivid it hurts my eyes, brightly coloured vegetables glowing like jewels against the dark earth. The man silently folds a pea pod into my hand and I split it open, scooping the tiny emerald treasures into my mouth; lightheaded, convulsing. Sweet freshness bursting on my tongue as I sink to the floor. I reach out and grab a fistful of salad leaves as if I'm drowning.

When it is over I stagger back through the woods, smeared with dirt and drunk on vitamins. *Leek. Runner bean. Endive. Onion.* I touch the packet of seeds in my pocket and know that there will be a second time.

The Moon Never Really Fades

This is the first time she has left the house without someone physically attached to her for over a year. She has laid her plans with pinpoint precision, waiting until the very last moment to breastfeed her daughter before handing over to her husband and sprinting out of the door. The countdown to when she slowly balloons with milk again has already begun.

The sun has barely risen, but the car has already taken on that fake-leather stink that manifests when the weather is warm. She rolls down the window and sticks her head out, like a dog. Considers howling.

She drives past uniform semi-detached houses, and in her peripheral vision she notices the fading moon, a faint thumbprint on blue. Last night's dream floods back: she had been tasked with picking the moon off the floor of a swimming pool. She had laboured, obedient, straining beneath its solemn weight, before succumbing to the lack of air and waking up gasping. She spent the next hour staring at her daughter, whose face glowed pale and round in the early dawn light.

She hopes it's not a premonition, because the pool is where she's headed. Once inside the damp-floored confinement of a cubicle she peels off sweaty clothes and tries not to think about verrucas. Her right breast is already starting to swell and dimple. She wonders what'll happen if she leaks into the pool: whether the milky trail will turn blue like when somebody pees, advertising the symbiotic relationship she now shares with her child. Like the moon, she must keep waxing and waning; filling up and running dry.

The water is a little too cold to be pleasant, the contrast with the humid air the most sharply pronounced as her pubic mound breaks the surface. Her gasp echoes around the crowded pool and she dunks the rest of herself in quickly, face burning. As she starts to kick and glide things improve. It does her good to be weightless, to feel the smooth caress of the water against her skin. To be touched on her own terms.

She flips onto her back and floats, observing the tiles on the ceiling; the black mould forming between the cracks. Out of the corner of her eye she sees a woman bob past. She is wearing a bright yellow swimming cap with a huge flower on it that must be half the size of her head. The floppy rubber absurdity of it combined with the woman's serene oblivion unlocks something deep inside her. She feels a hot tear slide down her cheek and trickle away into the water.

She wonders if this is where she's been going wrong: expecting happiness to be something she finds and settles into, once several unspecified things have been ticked off a list. Maybe it was only ever supposed to be fleeting moments plucked from the air like butterflies, then set free into the universe.

Maybe she needs to pay more attention to stupid yellow hats.

She swims harder, thrashing and kicking as if she can outswim the emptiness inside of her. One foot curls in the sudden agony of cramp, then the other, dragging her down. Her mouth opens in a gargled scream and water pours in. Black spots burst in front of her eyes and turn into moons, which then transform into her daughter's face. They kaleidoscope around her head, and she thinks: *Really? Even now?*

Then someone hauls her out and she lies on the cold chlorine floor, retching and spitting. Her breasts are granite-hard, throbbing against her swimsuit. As she is gently guided into the recovery position she sees the yellow hat lady walking slowly towards the changing rooms. She focuses on the bright, bobbing petals until they blur, then become stars. She tries to make the moment last.

Becoming

Since moving to the countryside, I have started to feed the birds. They have distinctly different personalities: the robin the most confident; the great tits skittish but aggressive when threatened; the wren elusive. The robin, in particular, is semi-tame, and approaches me even as I sit with the window open, observing the minute feathers around its eyes and the tremblingly delicate rise and fall of its puffed-out chest.

I order a *Guide to Birds of Britain and Ireland* and a pair of heavy-duty binoculars, and start to spend weekends in the woods. My joints grow stiff with lack of movement but I am ever more triumphant as I tick off great spotted woodpeckers, redwings, firecrests. At night I dream that I am a bird, wings stretched wide as I surf the breeze, nothing but the sky to cage me.

In some ways I have started to resent them; their freedom and detachment from a human world. Yes, the robin comes to me for crumbs in the morning, but he would do just as well without me. Here I am, forced to trudge to the shops to buy things, assemble meals. Compelled to comb my hair, clothe myself and perform a never-ending list of tasks that to me appear entirely arbitrary.

I consider how it would be to build a nest; somewhere to feel safe, to hunker down. So I gather up twigs and moss, constructing a neat oval. Just large enough. Once finished to my liking, I climb inside, burrowing in and embracing the sharp ends of twigs that scrape my skin, the feathers tickling my nose. I curl up in the foetal position and inhale the scent of soil and leaves and bark. When I look up all I can see is the tree canopy overhead, rustling gently in the breeze.

At night I lie restless, back in the bed that has never truly felt like mine. The artificial lavender scent of the sheets scratches at the back of my throat despite their last laundering being only a distant memory. Everything is too smooth, too clean, too synthetic, right down to my slippery faux-satin pyjamas that slide sweatily up my spine as I move. I open the window and soothe myself to sleep by watching the stars, the muted hoots of owls gently calling me home.

I decide that I will sleep in my nest; the nights are growing warmer. I feel excitement as I make my way into the woods, stepping carefully into yesterday's footprints. Dusk is falling as I reach the nest, partially concealed in the undergrowth; just as inviting as when I'd left it. With the night's silence interrupted only by the occasional snap of a twig as I adjust myself, I sleep better than I have done in weeks.

I wake early with the sunrise and luxuriate in the sound of birdsong; for once I feel part of it. A lone woodcock hops about in close proximity: it knows I am not a threat. I watch it pecking and scratching the ground, pulling up the occasional grub or worm with casual dexterity. My stomach rumbles. My jaw aches with curiosity and a sudden burst of saliva that arrives out of nowhere. I lurch forward, the bird taking off with a reproachful *pisssp*, and wriggle on my stomach towards the patch it was pecking at. I am close enough to smell the earth, to see each crumb of soil in hyper-real detail. I observe as a worm flails slowly, partially out of the ground from where the bird has disturbed it. I pinch the tip between finger and thumb and pull; it stretches, and just as I think it is going to break it slides out from the ground. I hold it in my palm and watch as it pulses and coils over and over.

All of a sudden it is in my mouth, more visceral than I could have imagined. I gnash my teeth across its squirming, fibrous body. I force myself to chew and swallow. Grits of earth choke my throat and tears sting the corners of my eyes. I realise that I am on all fours, limbs trembling.

As the sun rises I make my way back to the house for fresh clothes, to reluctantly brush my teeth. It is a beautiful day; the sky achingly blue. I watch a swallow flit across my peripheral vision, bobbing and wheeling in dizzying arcs, and feel a burst of frustration at the mundanity of the tasks I must perform even while taking these tentative steps towards freedom; my stupid, basic need to use a tin opener, avail myself of electricity, collect tampons.

The next evening it is warmer still. I experiment with taking off my leggings, then my T-shirt. My nipples harden and goose flesh prickles over my arms and legs as the night air makes contact with my skin. It is not unpleasant. Emboldened, I remove my underwear, and crouch naked in the undergrowth, feet splayed into the soil. I stay as still as I can, breathing shallow. Ants crawl up my legs; I pick them off and eat them, savouring the citrus burn across my tongue. I urinate and luxuriate in the glorious simplicity of it, steam rising from the golden puddle.

I sleep in the nest every night, amidst heaps of moss and dry ferns, becoming accustomed to the sensation of foliage against my bare skin. I indulge in the roulette of insect consumption, comparing the flinty crunch of beetles' shells with the barely-there sherbert pop of aphids. I place a blackbird's egg inside my vagina and hunch contentedly in my nest, feeling fuller than ever before.

And all the while the birds become ever more comfortable in my presence and now hop about alongside me as I go about my business, seeing me—at worst—as healthy competition for worms.

I return to the house intermittently, although my trips are becoming less frequent. I understand that I cannot survive only on insects, despite my best efforts. But birds are fed by humans, sometimes. My sporadic missions to pick up tins of baked beans and the odd cereal bar are merely the ornithological equivalents of winter-diminished sparrows pecking at a fat ball. I never linger for long.

Summer continues. I am tentatively happy; having cast off as many human trappings as possible, I feel myself unfolding. But I question whether this is enough, if it will ever be enough. I live like a bird as much as I can, but am hobbled by the elbowed, fleshy awkwardness of my arms that will never be able to fly. I watch my companions ascend into the infinite sky with an ache that weighs stone-heavy in my chest. My shoulder blades tingle with the wings I'll never have.

Day by day, I gather feathers; shed naturally by my companions. They are gifts, each one an acknowledgement of how far I've come. A necessarily gradual initiation. After several weeks I have a collection of over one hundred, all different types. I fetch sticks and vines, along with some rusty nails and a hammer I find in the basement of the house. I begin to weave together a frame to stretch the length of my arms and down my back, lashing the vines all over to provide a snug grid into which I can tuck the accumulated feathers. Finally, I make loops to put my arms into, and a string of ivy that ties tight under my breasts to secure the structure.

Standing up with the wings for the first time is disorientating in an exhilarating way. I spread my arms wide and the thrilling claustrophobia of not being able to move them in the way I could before is like the missing piece slotting into place; the slight ache from the restriction of the wooden supports almost pleasurable. My hands are no longer hands. I am one step closer.

I begin to feel the effects of living outside, exposed to the elements. Covered in dirt, cuts and bruises, my skin is a colour I no longer recognise. My feet have grown hard, thick soles; the ripe smell of my unwashed body hovers in my nostrils. My hip bones jut out and my stomach complains relentlessly, liquid swirling grumbles that soundtrack the process of my insides consuming themselves. When I clamber to my feet I feel faint, and my vision blurs so that the world around me is little more than a mass of hazy green.

I barely go back to the house at all now: it has started to scare me. But it is colder now, and I need matches. Today, I wake with the dawn under a bowl of birdsong, and set off through the woods at a furtive trot. I am wearing a tunic made from a sack with the legs and armholes cut out, stray feathers laced between the loose threads. And my wings; I seldom remove them.

As I approach the garden gate adrenaline jackknifes through my chest: there is someone at the front door. What sort of person are they? Something sparks in my memory and I realise it is a postman. It knocks on the door several times.

I am animal, afraid. I duck down and huddle behind a bush, the frightened creature of my heart threatening to escape from my mouth in my distress. This is the first human I have encountered for months, and it mustn't see me. My stomach rumbles and I tip to one side. My wings make it impossible for me to break my own fall and I roll onto my back where I lie stunned, as if I've just flown into a windowpane. The *scrunch-scrunch* of footsteps approaches and the postman's head appears over the wall. I watch its expression snap from mild confusion to horror. I twist, mustering strength from my wasted, dirt-blackened legs and heave myself into a sitting position. My mouth opens but all that comes out is a terrible jagged caw that sticks in my throat. The postman's own mouth mirrors mine, moving wordlessly in shock. Hefting myself sideways onto a wood-framed elbow, I push myself into a standing position and start to run, staggering at the pain in my cold-swollen joints. The postman finds its voice now, but I don't look back. I thrash through the woods without my usual practiced care, bouncing off tree trunks and stumbling over stray briars that tear at my ankles. I reach my nest and scramble to gather the pieces of who I thought I was. I am a bag of shaken-out feathers spiralling away on the wind. And now I've been spotted, I know I don't have long left.

The temperature drops further. Matchless, my attempts to start a fire with sticks and a rock are ineffectual, despite freeing my arms from my wings for a rare half an hour. They're back in place now, and I fold them around myself, shivering in my nest; holding the broken parts of myself together. The cold leaks into my bones and I settle into it, welcome numbness gradually replacing throbbing agony. Frost settles. I wonder whether I could unfold my limbs again, even if I wanted to. I close my eyes: I am an owl high above the trees looking down at this woman, framed in a perfect oval, pale and frozen. Finally free. I beat my wings and soar towards the stars.

Nancy

When Nancy turned into a sunflower it came as a surprise: she was generally not the sort of person to which unusual things happened. But one morning—it hadn't even been that long ago—she'd woken to the feeling that her pillow had become extremely uncomfortable overnight. As she sat up, a sudden swoop of yellow in her peripheral vision had her running to the mirror, where she found that thick petals had sprouted all around her face. She raised a tentative hand, which was now a leaf, and watched as her reflection did the same. The petals were smooth to the touch; delicate but substantial, as if it would be a job to pluck them off.

It wasn't just her face that had changed. Her body, formerly unremarkable in a comforting sort of way, was now a thick, unbendable stem. Her skin had turned green and tough, with soft, itchy hairs coating her from top to bottom. Her lower legs and feet had become gnarled roots which dragged horribly, forcing her to shuffle along like a reluctant participant in a three-legged race.

Inevitably, this raised questions.

"How'm I supposed to have sex with a sunflower?" her husband had wanted to know.

"I think that's the least of our worries, Jeff," she'd muttered with as much dignity as an oversized plant could muster.

Yes, there were certain practicalities to being a sunflower that Nancy hadn't previously envisaged. Her teeth turned into seeds and would periodically fall out in the middle of speaking, cascading from her mouth when she least expected it. This made her very popular with squirrels, a devoted band of whom now followed her about. They weren't too bad, although were proving to be very disruptive in meetings. Nancy had lost count of the times where she'd opened her mouth to make a particularly dynamic point, only to be upstaged by the staccato clatter of seeds skidding across the table with a gang of eager rodents in hot pursuit. As per the HR guidelines, Nancy's employers were officially supportive of her newfound state, but naturally, she wasn't immune to her colleagues' eye rolls and smirks of derision. What had been formally stated on paper didn't protect her from the cold feeling in the pit of her stomach when she realised that she'd not been invited out for lunch, again, or when she was asked to turn off her camera on Zoom while everyone else got to keep theirs on.

Her son Finn, at least, was accepting—*truly* accepting, not like at work. It had surprised her, actually. He was nine, so old enough to start realising she wasn't cool anymore; old enough to feel embarrassed at her very existence, even in human form. But he'd just sighed, and hugged her awkwardly around the stem, before leaping away—"you're all fuzzy!"

"But I'm still me," she'd said, smiling as hard as she could as tears threatened to spill from her scratchy seed-husk eyes.

"'Course you are," he replied. "Can we get pizza?"

Nancy agreed gratefully, especially given that having leaves as arms meant that cooking had become something of a difficulty. Jeff, of course, performatively threw his share in the bin, sighing elaborately and banging the door on his way out. Finn ate double the amount out of solidarity, his round face silent and determined as he chewed and swallowed. The squirrels watched on in anticipation.

If Nancy was being honest with herself, her recent metamorphosis hadn't come as a *total* shock. There had been signs; she just hadn't wanted to think about what they meant. The unusual yellow streak in her hair. The tooth that had suddenly gone brown and pointy, leaving her dentist nonplussed. The hairs on her legs turning green. There had been a period of time, before, when Jeff's gradual turning away from her had been crushing; had made her wilt and waste. But as her son had grown older and she'd started to see what a good person he was turning out to be, something began to change. Every cruel dig from her husband caused another petal to sprout mentally, another patch of green to bloom and spread. She had started to think seriously about leaving, for Finn at least. The seeds of rebellion had started to take root, and new shoots unfurled just a little more each day, one millimetre at a time. *Not yet, but soon.*

It turned out that soon arrived quicker than she'd thought it would.

Nancy had known it was going to be a bad day since the night before, when Jeff had crashed in after midnight with no explanation. In bed, he'd rolled her roughly towards him, before grunting in disgust and pushing her away.

Finn had gone off early to school, as he often did these days; his cereal bowl and spoon lay rinsed on the draining board. Her heart twisted and flared at the sight of it. She didn't know where he'd got this solid core of *goodness* from; it seemed almost unfathomable that amidst the frankly dysfunctional emotional environment he was being brought up in that he was such a sensitive, thoughtful person. Perhaps it was the ultimate act of defiance against his father.

Nancy took a glass down from the cupboard, cupping her leaves around its circumference with the precise caution of a toddler. She placed it in the sink and began the process of trying to turn the tap on. She couldn't call for Jeff, because seeing her flounder with this sort of thing would only make him angry. She eased the faucet around gently, slowly, trying not to tear her leaves as they strained against the metal. Nearly, nearly. She had almost done it, a single, pendulous drop of water trembling at the mouth of the tap, and she pushed, pushed some more, and as it finally yielded the force of her efforts spun her into the crockery drying on the draining board. The whole awkward weight of her skidded everything onto the floor where it bounced, rolled and shattered in every direction while a plume of water streamed into the now-abandoned glass in the sink.

"You fucking useless bitch." She hadn't realised he was there. Maybe he'd been watching her the whole time.

It happened so quickly, but she glimpsed the clouded fury in his eyes and the flash of metal as he swiped; heard the *snick* before she felt a thing. Didn't understand what had happened until she saw one of her leaves on the floor and noticed the dribble of clear goo seeping from the site of the wound. Seeds tumbled as her mouth fell open in an oval of surprise. Jeff looked shocked at himself, face crumbling like dry earth. He stared at the scissors as if they'd acted of their own accord. But he didn't say sorry, or pick up the fallen leaf, or tell her that he wished he could have taken it back. And as they stared at each other in that long, unbroken moment with the tap gushing in the background, Nancy's resolve crystallised. She turned and made her way towards the garden.

It was raining, but the morning sun sliced cartoonish stripes through the clouds: rainbow weather. She staggered outside, and as her roots made contact with the soil they curled involuntarily, as comfortable as if she'd stepped into a favourite pair of shoes. Nancy broke into an awkward trot, the pain in her side causing her to move with greater urgency as she hobbled out of the garden gate. She would have to go get Finn. The screech of the patio door had her turning back around, and she nearly toppled over at the sight that greeted her.

"Mum!" Finn's seed-studded face was scrunched up. "I'm coming with you." Nancy took in the raggedy yellow mane standing out around his head, his lanky, green stem.

"What are you still doing here?"

Finn shook his head, petals swaying.

"I woke up like this today, so I hid," he whispered. "I'm sorry, Mum." They wobbled towards each other, collided in an embrace.

"Let's go," whispered Nancy.

Due to the hour and the weather they didn't see many people, although a few dog walkers did a double take as they lurched past with the squirrels scampering after them. They didn't stop until they reached open fields with woodland beyond. Nancy led the way towards a sheltered spot beside a thicket of trees and felt herself relax into the earth, a full-body exhalation. She dug in. The sense of relief was so intense she felt herself sagging, but when she looked down, she realised that she was standing straighter than she had in years. Finn, less sure of himself in his new form, searched her face for guidance as he planted into the soil beside her, his face opening with delight as he settled and took root.

"We did it, Mum," he whispered.

They touched leaves and turned their faces towards the sun.

Acknowledgements

First of all, a huge thank you to Isabelle Kenyon, for taking a chance on my stories: I am incredibly grateful!

Thank you to the organisers of the Roehampton Creative Writing Competition 2019 - David Fallon, Amy Waite and the team of student interns at Fincham Press. Thank you to Leone Ross, who gave me my first print publication in the student anthology. The whole experience was instrumental in helping me believe that I was a writer, and gave me the push to take it seriously. I can honestly say that this particular book would not be in existence without you all!

Huge thanks to the members of the B&B Writing Group, who have all at some point or another provided feedback on one or more of these stories, and been a constant source of encouragement and all around good eggs. Particular thanks to Matt Kendrick, Michelle Christophorou, Laura Besley and James Montgomery.

Thank you to the wider writing community I have found on Twitter - it may be a bin out there but my life would genuinely be poorer without knowing you! You all know who you are, but a special shoutout must go to Barbara Byar and HLR for their friendship and salient writing advice.

Thank you to Damien, for the kindness and love, and always supporting me to follow my dreams.

And finally, thank you to Francis: you have stolen my sleep but inspired me to write, and to live the life I've always wanted.

About the Author

Katie Oliver is a writer based on the west coast of Ireland, whose work has been nominated for the Pushcart Prize, Best Small Fictions and Best Microfiction. I WANTED TO BE CLOSE TO YOU is her debut short story collection. She can be found on Twitter @katie_rose_o

Previously published

Many thanks to the below publishers and magazines for finding homes for my work.

'Tending the Garden'/'Spider Season'/'Gum Leaf Skeletoniser'/'At the Top of the House' - *Reflex Fiction*, March 2020/July 2020/March 2021/April 2020
'Together we grow' - *X-R-A-Y*, March 2021
'Hold on tight' - *Funny Pearls*, February 2020
'TimeOut'/'All That Glitters' - *Fincham Press,* October 2019/May 2021
'When She Laid an Egg' - *Nurture Literary*, July 2021
The Moon Never Really Fades be added' - *Ellipsis Zine*, January 2022

About Fly on the Wall Press

A publisher with a conscience.
Political, Sustainable, Ethical.
Publishing politically-engaged, international fiction, poetry and cross-genre anthologies on pressing issues. Founded in 2018 by founding editor, Isabelle Kenyon.

Some other publications:

The Woman With An Owl Tattoo by Anne Walsh Donnelly
The Prettyboys of Gangster Town by Martin Grey
The Sound of the Earth Singing to Herself by Ricky Ray
Inherent by Lucia Orellana Damacela
Medusa Retold by Sarah Wallis
Pigskin by David Hartley
We Are All Somebody
Aftereffects by Jiye Lee
Someone Is Missing Me by Tina Tamsho-Thomas
*Odd as F*ck by Anne Walsh Donnelly*
Muscle and Mouth by Louise Finnigan
Modern Medicine by Lucy Hurst
These Mothers of Gods by Rachel Bower
Sin Is Due To Open In A Room Above Kitty's by Morag Anderson
Fauna by David Hartley
How To Bring Him Back by Clare HM
Hassan's Zoo and A Village in Winter by Ruth Brandt
No One Has Any Intention of Building A Wall by Ruth Brandt
Snapshots of the Apocalypse by Katy Wimhurst
Demos Rising
Exposition Ladies by Helen Bowie
A Dedication to Drowning by Maeve McKenna

Social Media:

@fly_press (Twitter) @flyonthewall_poetry (Instagram)
@flyonthewallpress (Facebook)
www.flyonthewallpress.co.uk